To Lorrie, Jennifer and Joanna...thank you!

Sip and SAVOR

sip and savor

BELLA MICHAELS

CHAPTER ONE

min

Kitchi Falls, Finger Lakes, NY

"My nephew is one of those—what do you call them? Naked dancers?"

Dorothy reached across the counter, taking my money as if she had not just said "naked dancers." The town gossip and retired schoolteacher had surprised me many times over the years, but this one took the cake.

"Um, do you mean male entertainer?" I ventured, not one hundred percent comfortable with this conversation's major U-turn. We were talking about my sister-in-law's bachelorette party, which of course, the co-owner of Devine Bakery had already heard about. And then, boom! Naked dancers.

"Sounds like a fancy word for a stripper. That's what I meant to say." Dorothy handed me a bag of cinnamon donuts and my change, which I promptly tossed in the tip jar.

"I had no idea you had a nephew in Nashville."

"I'd be surprised if your paths hadn't crossed," she said. "He was here for almost a month one summer."

"I don't think I remember him." Granted, my bad memory was only one of my many faults.

"It was a long time ago," she said as the tinkling sound of a bell above the door announced a new customer. "I think you were both in middle school."

"Morning, Dorothy," a new voice called. "Dominica. Always good to see you. Like two rays of sunshine."

Dorothy stepped out of the way as Rob Smith moved to the counter. A good friend of Dominca's father and owner of half the town, including the grocery store next door, he was as much a staple of the community as Dorothy and her husband, Rich.

"I was just telling Dominica about my nephew," Dorothy said, "a singer in Nashville." Giving me a sharp look I interpreted as *keep the stripper thing quiet,* she continued doing what she did best. Spill the tea. "Dominica and some of the girls are going down there for a bachelorette party this weekend. Can you imagine? I didn't even have a bachelorette party, never mind getting on a plane to Nashville for it. Kids these days."

She acted as if my friends and I were fresh out of high school. Of all my friends, I was the youngest at twenty-five, not exactly a kid anymore.

"You're always on the go," Rob said. "I thought your mother was a firecracker, but you're the busiest of the bunch, aren't you?"

An understatement. "That's what they say."

"Your dad was just telling me they never see you these days."

I tried hard not to roll my eyes. That sounded just like my dad. "He was literally at the winery two days this week. And as the only sibling still actually living with my parents, I'd say he sees me more than most."

My dad was still having a hard time with retirement. It would be a year this spring since he and Mom passed the family winery on to my siblings and me, but the adjustment was proving difficult for him. Understandable, since he'd built it from the ground up.

"Don't shoot the messenger," Rob said.

Attempting to change the subject, I tried to escape. "I have to get these back to the vineyard before I get a hangry text from Thayle, who's covering the Wine Barn for me."

"Tell Antonio's girl I said hello."

Antonio's girl. Honestly, sometimes it seemed like we were still living in the 1950s in this town.

"Don't go without Hudson's number," Dorothy said, stopping me. I couldn't tell her in front of Rob that I didn't need it. Pretty sure saying *We already have tickets to a male revue, but thank you very much* would raise an eyebrow, not to mention I'd be spilling Dorothy's secret. She had nothing to be ashamed of, but since Rob Smith had a standing poker night with my father, advertising our Nashville itinerary, including the male revue, wasn't on my to-do list today.

"Is your brother ready to get hitched?" Rob asked as Dorothy wrote down her nephew's number on a business card. I briefly considered telling her she could text it to me but then nixed the idea as I stared at the old-fashioned cash register on the counter.

"My parents are ready for him to marry, that's for sure. They're still afraid Brooke will change her mind. He can be tough sometimes."

Rob waved his hand in dismissal. "I don't believe that for a second. I haven't met a Grado who's anything but charming, Cosimo included." We locked eyes and began laughing at the same time. "Okay," he amended, "I'll admit Marco is also a bit of a handful."

Rob was one of the only people who used our full names instead of nicknames. And he was right on that point, Marco was charming for sure. Maybe too much, though. "Bit of a handful? I think you're forgetting the time he put your bar's muscat in his pickup and took it to the football field."

"That one is hard to forget," he said as Dorothy handed the card to me.

"But to be fair," she chimed in, "my son instigated that particular prank. And it was quite a few years ago."

"He hasn't matured much," I said of my brother. "But to answer your question, Cos is more than ready. And we're thrilled to have Brooke as a part of the family."

"One dozen cinnamon, please," Rob said to Dorothy. "She seems like a really nice woman. Your dad adores her."

"We all do," I said sincerely. "Thanks for this." I lifted up the card to Dorothy. "We'll be sure to connect with him. To hear his . . . music." I gave her a conspiratorial wink, and for a change, she was on the defensive. Usually, Dorothy was like a pit bull using Devine Bakery as a front for gossip collecting.

I turned over the card. Hudson Parker. Without the heart to tell her we probably wouldn't connect since one male revue in five days was probably enough, I slipped the Devine Bakery card into my purse and thanked her, preparing to snag a cinnamon donut well before I arrived back to the estate.

CHAPTER TWO

hudson

"I'D KILL FOR THAT," I SAID.

We watched Donny head out the back door hand in hand with his wife. Unlike most of the guys at Encore, he was properly hitched and happy about it. Truth be told, I envied the guy.

"You've got to be kidding me." Oliver packed up with most of the guys heading out for the night, but I had another gig to get to. "One woman for the rest of your life. Think about it."

That earned Oliver a snicker from the others. I had been working with Encore for nearly two years, and while these guys could be boneheads, I counted them all as friends, even though they knew full well I wasn't just like them. Being fawned over by women who saw nothing but a six-pack and no brains in my head wasn't my idea of a good time. Not that the women I danced for would ever know it. I took my job as seriously as possible given the nature of it. The women came here for a good time. To blow off steam, get away from their real lives for a few hours, and I delivered.

But that didn't mean working as a male entertainer lent itself to meeting the woman of my dreams. Far from it.

"Where you headed? Maybe we'll come with you," Oliver said.

"Outlaw." I smiled.

"No, thanks," he said, slapping me on the shoulder. "You're on your own. Are you closing it down?"

"Yep." I couldn't resist ribbing my friend a little. "Should I tell Shayla you said hello?"

"You can be a real asshole sometimes."

Looked like Oliver and the pretty bartender at Outlaw Alehouse were not getting back together anytime soon.

Snickering, I finished packing up. "Guilty as charged."

"Speaking of being guilty, I heard what you did for that bachelorette from Thursday night. Class act, man. How did it happen?"

Slinging my guitar over one shoulder and a gym bag over the other, I shrugged. I was usually off on Thursdays, but this week the bar downstairs was short-staffed. In addition to this gig, and playing guitar wherever I could get the stage, I occasionally picked up a few bartending hours too. Which was how I'd gotten roped into an impromptu striptease for a bachelorette party at the bar.

"I overheard someone ask why she wasn't upstairs at the male revue. There was no mistaking her as anything other than a bride," Oliver said.

"Sash?"

"And crown."

"What did she say?"

I thought back to two nights ago. "She said they couldn't afford it. That she begged her friends not to go overboard, to save their money for the wedding."

"But she could afford a bachelorette party in Nashville?"

"Locals," I said.

"Locals? On Broadway? That's strange."

"I thought so too, but apparently one of the women was an out-of-towner, so they were showing her the strip."

"So you felt bad, pumped up the music and gave the woman a complimentary dance?"

I smiled, remembering her expression when I'd hopped on the bar in front of her. "I did."

"Got himself a nice slap on the wrist," added Mike, our resident dancing firefighter, both on the stage and in real life.

We had a license to perform up here, above the bar, for the show. Not so much below. But it was worth it. She and her friends thanked me a hundred times.

"Shit." Oliver had gone to the door, opened it, and shut it so quickly every one of us knew who was on the other side of that door.

"Who's she here for?" Mike asked.

At least every other night a woman, or an entire group of women if we were especially unlucky, waited for one of the guys at our back entrance.

"Who do you think?" Oliver looked pointedly at me.

"Parker," Mike said. "Always Parker."

The other guys laughed.

"Is she hot?" one of them asked.

"Doesn't matter," I said. "I've got to get to Outlaw."

Oliver sighed before I could even ask him to talk to them. I sighed in relief, because I did have a gig to get to, but more importantly, I really didn't want to deal with these women. Some of the others had no problem turning the overzealous women away, but for me, it was my least favorite part of the job. I was here to make a few bucks and put a smile on some faces, not to let them down.

"I owe you one," I said to him, heading toward the front. I figured by now the stage area would be cleared out. If I was lucky, I could sneak out by taking the stairs down to the bar and heading right out the front door. And if not . . . I was about to potentially get mobbed by a few dozen horny women.

CHAPTER THREE

min

"SERIOUSLY, YOU TWO."

I had endured enough of the PDA-packed goodbye sessions. Between Cos and Brooke earlier this morning, and now my brother Neo and his fiancée Thayle, the tasting room had turned into some Poconos couples resort. At least we weren't open yet.

"I'll meet you in the Barn," I said to Thayle, as if anyone was listening. Neo and Thayle were too wrapped up in their long goodbye, which might have made more sense if we were leaving for a month instead of a five-day-long weekend.

Preparing to be blasted with frigid January air as I opened the door, I pulled my hood up and dashed across the courtyard to the Barn. I tried not to kill myself on freshly fallen snow as I made my way up the stairs to the Barn, passing the massive "Welcome to Grado Valley Vineyards" sign, and then I whipped open the door.

"Holy shit, you scared me," I said.

The bride-to-be stood behind the tasting counter, working as usual.

"Sorry. I just wanted to get a few last-minute emails out," Brooke said.

Unlike the Wine Cellar, where I left Neo and Thayle about to make a baby in the middle of the damn room, the 1931 Wine Barn, or just "the Barn" as we called it, was more intimate. Whereas the 1942 Wine Cellar was a huge, wide-open space with vaulted ceilings, my home away from home was decorated to emulate a Tuscan converted barn. With its rustic-looking elements both indoors and out, the courtyard, beautiful at night with white bulb lights criss-crossing the shrub-enclosed area, this was actually the second most-rented spot for engagements and wedding pictures on the property.

"Wayne will be here any second." I scurried to my office to grab a few things and then headed back out to find Brooke putting on her jacket.

"You didn't have to get us a driver," Brooke said. "Cos could have taken us to the airport."

"He'd be more likely to pretend to get lost and make us miss the flight. I swear I've never seen my brother like this before. You'd swear you were leaving him until next June."

Beautiful Brooke—as I liked to think of her in my head, because she was—grinned widely. Apparently, she liked the idea of Cosimo missing her like crazy. "It's the first time we've been apart since the summer."

When Brooke and her friends had come to GVV for a wine tasting last summer, none of us, least of all Brooke, had imagined we'd end up here, a month before her winter wedding to my brother. She'd been living in Manhattan at the time and, to be honest, she and Cos didn't really hit it off when they first met. Now she was the marketing director for the vineyard, with an office just down the hallway from Cos, and hands down it was the happiest I'd ever seen him in my life.

But this weekend was not about Cos. "Well, get used to it. Because this is a girls' weekend. A bachelorette party to end all bachelorette parties. No boy talk."

"You're scaring me." Brooke packed up her laptop with a look on her face much like Thayle's whenever she spied Devine Bakery's cinnamon donuts. Brooke had promised to leave the laptop home. No boy talk or working. But she seemed to be having second thoughts.

"You should be scared," I told her. Brooke could party with the best of them, and I was determined to make her and her friends proud. They'd helped Thayle and me prepare for the weekend's shenanigans, and I knew Brooke couldn't wait to see her friends when we landed in Nashville.

"Speaking of boy talk—"

"No," I said before she could continue. "Especially not him."

Just before Christmas I met a guy from the neighboring town at KC's Taphouse. A handful of dates later, I brought him home to meet the family and have regretted it ever since. My brothers hadn't liked any guy I ever dated, and David was no exception. We parted ways a few weeks ago when he told me I spent way too much time with my family. To be honest, he was right. But I liked my family, and we were business partners, making it sort of unavoidable that we hung out more often than not. Plus, my best friend was also now my brother's fiancée, so . . . David's loss.

"I know you really liked him," Brooke said.

"I liked kissing him," I admitted.

Brooke laughed. "You're a nut."

"And you," I scolded, "are *not* taking that." I literally snatched my future sister-in-law's laptop bag from her and headed to the door where, perfect timing, Thayle and Neo had just walked in.

"Take this." I shoved Brooke's laptop at my brother. "When Cos gets back, give it to him. Tell him to lock it up because"—I turned to glare at Brooke, who was making a face at me—"the bride-to-be is a workaholic."

Neo took the bag. "One which I'm sure you'll help her with this weekend. Just please don't get anyone into trouble."

"If by anyone you mean Thayle, you can just stop it right there. She was my partner in crime before she was your girlfriend."

"Fiancée."

"Whatever."

Thayle walked over to the window, most likely to watch out for our driver, leaving me to argue with Neo, one of my favorite pastimes.

"So what do you have planned?" he whispered.

"You tell me first." I already knew the boys' plans thanks to Marco, but Neo didn't know our other brother had told me anything.

"You know, just hanging out. Guy stuff."

I crossed my arms. "If by 'guy stuff' you mean the titty bar in Seneca Falls, then yeah, I know what you mean."

Neo's eyes widened at that a second before they narrowed. "Marco told you."

"Was it supposed to be a secret?"

He shrugged.

"Does Thayle know?"

Neo's smugness was my least favorite of his qualities.

"Yes, Thayle knows. And trusts me implicitly. I wish I could say the same about you."

I deliberately misunderstood. "Thayle trusts me just fine."

"Limo's here," Thayle yelled, the excitement in her voice mirroring my own. It was unseasonably warm at the moment in Nashville, and more than anything else, we were ready to ditch these winter coats, feel some sun on our faces, and party like it was 1999.

"Do not put your drinks down," Neo said to all three of us. "And don't walk back to the hotel alone."

"House," I said. "We have a rental house."

"Whatever. Just please be careful."

"Always." I blew my brother a kiss and headed over toward the bar where my luggage was waiting. He said goodbye to Thayle, again, and we were finally on our way. The limo awaited, as did the promise of a fun, uncomplicated weekend with no ex-boyfriends to worry about, no brothers to steal away my girls' attention, and a hell of a lot of drinks to drink.

I opened the front door of my beloved Barn. In truth, I couldn't chastise Brooke much, as I typically worked seven days a week. But I didn't mind. Grado was in my blood, and I loved seeing it soar. But this weekend would be all play and no work, and I was ready to get started.

CHAPTER FOUR

hudson

"There you are. Jesus, Hudson, you're gonna kill yourself," Donny said.

I didn't deny it. This was cutting it a bit close even for me.

"Sorry I missed pregaming," I said, tearing off my shirt and jeans. There was no modesty back here. In ten seconds flat, I was out of my bartender's clothes and heading for the costume rack.

"No problem." Donny was already sporting a slew of dollar bills and the show hadn't even started. Usually, they made the guys work their way through the crowd, warming it up and giving the ladies a taste of what was to come. This second floor of the Whiskey Soul Saloon had its own bar, a stage, and enough room for around eighty customers. Encore's manager had taken us all around the country, but for the past two years we'd stayed here in Nashville, performing at Whiskey Soul. The Nashville bachelorette party game was strong. Our manager rarely attended shows since we all knew the routine: Get out there, let them see our faces and pick a favorite, then make it rain. The goal was for customers to forget the contents of their bank accounts and shower us with dollar bills.

"Officer Hudson," Oliver said, coming backstage. "You're up in two."

I had two songs to get ready, but I didn't need the prep. I put on a hat and began sifting through the props trunk, looking for handcuffs. "Where the hell are they?"

"I saw Oliver with them last night," someone joked. "Smuggled them out with him."

Finally, I found the handcuffs under some folded handkerchiefs inside the trunk, and I smiled at Oliver. "Thanks for putting them back."

"I've got my own," he said cheekily. "Don't need yours."

Laughter from the guys greeted me as the music started. It might have been a dysfunctional family, half naked as we were and smothered in scented oil, but we were a family nonetheless. When I came down to Nashville, hoping to make it big with my music, I never in a million years imagined myself here. I wasn't sure how long I'd last at Encore, but for the time being, it served a purpose.

"Big bachelorette party in the VIP section," Dominic said. "Some cuties in there."

"Your wife would like to hear that," Mike quipped.

"My wife is in the audience, thank you very much."

"Ouch," I said, trying to imagine how that conversation would go later. "I thought she didn't like to see you perform?"

"Oh, she likes to see me perform, alright. Just not usually here, in the club."

More laughter. I was ready, just waiting for my turn now.

"I don't think I could do it. Dance in front of my girlfriend," Oliver said.

"You don't have a girlfriend," I reminded him.

"Parker," the new guy just offstage called to me. "You're next."

"At least you got to dance before Parker," Mike muttered to the new guy as I made my way to the curtain that separated us from the main room. Because it was a bar, we entered from the back, walking through the crowd to the stage.

I was used to the ribbing. The guys complained when they went on after me, which was why I was usually on last. Tonight, however, I had to skip out early for a singing gig. I hated to leave here early, as this bar was one of the most popular in town and it brought in more than decent tips.

From here I could see the audience only from the back, with most of the women turned toward the stage. Watching the show, I thought about the first time I'd gotten up there. I'd just finished a set at Outlaw Ale House when Oliver introduced himself to me, said that if I ever wanted to make a few extra bucks, I had the "perfect look" for a gig that paid well.

The asshole never mentioned I'd be taking my clothes off.

Always up for a challenge though, I figured I'd give it a shot. A month later, I was working for Encore almost as much as I was singing, the real reason I'd come to Nashville in the first place.

Smiling as the ladies cheered, my gaze was drawn to the VIP section to the right of the stage. Something was happening, but I couldn't tell what exactly. The ladies weren't watching the show but instead were all huddled together. That was odd.

A few seconds later, one of women leapt off a barstool of the high-top where the group was seated, and another of them ran after her. Looked like they were heading to the ladies' room. The bride sat on the end, a perfect position for me to give her the extra attention her friends had paid for with their tickets in that section.

And then she turned toward him, apparently looking for her friends.

"Holy fuck," I muttered.

Mike sidled up to me. "What is it?"

"The VIP section. Bride, turned toward the bathroom."

Mike whistled. "She looks like that girl from *The Originals*." I was only half listening. "My ex was obsessed with that show. After, I don't know, like a hundred seasons of *The Vampire Diaries*, I had to sit through a spin-off. Not fun."

"What the hell are you talking about?" I said, his words having finally registered.

"The bride. She looks sort of like the half wolf, half vampire girl. Elijah's girlfriend. I mean, they never really got together for long but . . ." Mike stopped when the bride finally turned back to face the stage and I was able to pull my eyes from her to look askance at him.

"So you didn't like the show? You had me fooled."

He shrugged. "I guess it wasn't that bad."

I had no idea who the half wolf/half vampire was, but this woman was drop-dead gorgeous: Long dark hair. Eyes that I could tell must be brown even from across the room. And her lips—they couldn't be natural.

When the song ended, I snapped out of my fog. She was taken, engaged to be married. And now I really didn't want to dance for her. Indulging an attraction to customers was a big no-no, especially ones with a big white sash around their body. But she'd paid for it—or her friends did, at least —so I supposed I was going to have to suck it up and give the woman a lap dance.

Here went nothing.

CHAPTER FIVE

min

"THIS IS THE SONG FROM *MAGIC MIKE*," TINA SAID NEXT TO ME. Brooke's friend was one of my favorites. Actually, I liked all of Brooke's friends. Too bad my poor sister-in-law wasn't here to enjoy them.

"Are you sure we should stay?" Thayle asked.

"If we all missed out, Brooke would feel even worse," Amy said. Another friend of Brooke's, she had just gotten into town that morning. Unlike the rest of us who were still hurting from yesterday's drinking spree, Amy was raring to go.

"I can't believe Jen is missing out too, though," Amy said. "She was really looking forward to this."

When Brooke had tossed her sash around me, saying, "Enjoy the lap dances," I had been too stunned to know what was happening at first. Apparently, the hangover she'd thought had gone away had reared its ugly head again. Leeta, another of Brooke's friends who was also feeling the effects of going a touch too hard after we landed yesterday, had followed her into the bathroom. And then we got their text in the group chat: *Going home. Don't you dare leave.*

"Say hello to Mateo, ladies," the announcer boomed into the microphone.

"Holy Mary, Mother of god."

Tina had always had a way with words.

I turned to face the back of the room, where a cop was now making his way up the aisle to the stage, half sauntering, half dancing. And it wasn't his police uniform everyone stared at. Now that was a male entertainer. The other two guys we'd watched tonight weren't bad looking, but this one was almost as drop-dead gorgeous as Channing Tatum himself.

"If you told me to picture the perfect male stripper in my head, he's exactly what I would imagine. And will continue to do so probably for the rest of my life."

We all laughed at Amy, but she wasn't far off. And he could move too.

We weren't the only ones thinking it. There was a fresh round of screaming as he made his way to the stage. One second, the Greek god was fully clothed. The next, his pants were ripped off, revealing thick, muscled legs. Some guys didn't bother working out the bottom half at the gym, but he clearly wasn't one of them.

"I wonder what the guys are doing right now?" Thayle asked.

That was when I realized she'd completely lost her mind. "Are you seeing him right now? How could you care for a hot second what the guys, aka Neo, are doing right now?"

Oh boy. And now the shirt was off. Just boots, a black thong, a belt with handcuffs hanging from it, and a hat. That was it.

About the same time that everyone in the place began freaking out, he looked at me. Of course, he was paid to make every woman in the place feel special. But for one split second, I could have sworn he gave me *that* look. And then he was dancing again.

"Oh my god. He's coming over here," Amy said. And he was. "Min, he's coming for you."

Sure enough, I found myself being pulled off the barstool. Before I could say boo, he'd pulled me to the wall next to the girls, and he not-so-gently spun me around. Taking each wrist and splaying my hands above my head against the wall, he began an extremely thorough strip search.

I could hear the girls laughing hysterically. I, on the other hand, was pretending there wasn't a massive bulge pressed up against my ass cheeks. His hands slid from my arms down to my waist, and while he ground against me, I remembered the bride's own mantra. The first time I heard Brooke and her friends use the expression, I knew they were kindred spirits.

Seize the fucking day.

Flinging aside my mortification, I leaned into it. Or into him, more precisely, as Mateo finished his search.

"Looks like I have to bring you in," he whispered with a velvety smooth voice as sexy as his entertainer persona.

Spinning me back around, he guided me back to my barstool. But I turned to discover Mateo still standing there waiting for me to sit. I climbed onto the seat, probably as elegantly as a giraffe might if it had to hop onto a stool after that encounter, and watched as my police friend made a show of pulling out his cuffs.

Everyone, including my girls, lost it.

"I can't—" Thayle was laughing so hard I was sure she was about to pee her pants.

A police siren rang out, mixed with the music, as Mateo, standing behind me, grabbed both my hands and cuffed me to the back of the stool.

"Can he do that?" I asked Amy frantically over the music as her jaw dropped.

Moving back around to the front, Mateo answered. "Yes. I can."

I couldn't really do much about the fact that he proceeded to spread my legs apart. And then he was there, between them, grinding. I tried not to look down, but too late I realized my brain wasn't quite functioning correctly. There were nearly a hundred women in here who wanted to be me right now.

Enjoy it while it lasts.

So I did. I drunk my fill, so to speak. I took in every ab muscle, wishing my hands were free so I could feel them. I understood that he had to look good for a living, but his body was like something from a movie.

And just like that, the song was over. The girls were shoving dollars into Mateo's thong on my behalf, and then he moved to the back of my stool and uncuffed my hands. Assuming he'd gone already, I closed my legs and sat up, reaching for my drink.

"Too bad you're getting married," he whispered from behind. My head whipped back, but he was gone. As his perfect ass cheeks made their way down the aisle, he was inundated with dollars. Every so often he tipped his hat in thanks or reached out to make physical contact with women who seemed to have no problem reciprocating.

I couldn't blame them. Would've done the same if I could have.

Too bad you're getting married.

"Poor Brooke," Debby said. "She really missed out."

"Holy shit, Dominica. Are you okay?" someone asked. I had no idea who. Because no, I wasn't okay. Probably never would be again.

"He thought I was the bride," I mumbled. "That's why he picked me."

"Well, yeah." Tina grabbed my arm. "Don't look now, but it looks like there's a fire."

Vaguely I heard the new song, but when I looked back, Mateo was gone. In his place, a fireman. Though he didn't hold a candle to his predecessor.

"I wonder if all of the other guys hate Mateo for being so good looking?" Amy asked.

"I'll tell you one person who doesn't hate him." Leeta winked at me as the others laughed.

No, I didn't hate him at all. Not that it mattered, since I'd never see the guy again.

CHAPTER SIX

hudson

"Do I have any Kenny Chesney fans in here?"

The burgeoning crowd at my favorite bar on the strip clapped. The unusually warm January weather had brought out crowds more typical of spring. The windows behind me were open, letting in a cool breeze to offset the heat of a few hundred bodies singing along to my tunes.

"Alright then, here's to knowing you."

As I struck the first chords of a song I knew so well I could sing it in my sleep, my thoughts wandered. When I first came down here two years ago, the idea of "making it big" had seemed far off, but still a possibility. Now, not so much. I was booked solid with more headliners than most, but that elusive record deal was looking more and more like a pipe dream.

Funny thing about it, I wasn't sure I cared. Music had always been in my blood, a way to get to know myself and the world better. But the more I had to show up to play on someone else's schedule, the less singing and playing guitar felt like a passion. It was a job now, and honestly that sucked the joy out of it for me.

Still, it made people happy. It paid the bills. So for now, playing in this bar in the middle of Broadway on a Saturday afternoon was just fine.

As my fingers strummed the guitar my father had shockingly bought me just before I left New York, they walked in. The bride from last night. The same one I'd pictured in my shower this morning—leading me to curse myself for having done so. She was engaged, after all. Although it wasn't like I was screwing her. Not in real life, anyway.

There was something about her that drew me in. As her group looked for seats—good luck in here on a warm Saturday afternoon—and somehow snagged at least enough stools at the bar for half of their group, I kept my eyes on her.

She wore jeans and cowboy boots, likely ones she picked up in town. These were no real cowgirls, but Northern ladies come to Tennessee for a good time. Didn't matter. The boots looked so good on her that she could break as many fashion rules as she wanted. Tourist? Maybe. Hot as fucking hell? Definitely.

Finishing the song to the tempered kind of applause a slow song usually elicits, I raised my hand and thanked the crowd.

"Stick with me, folks. I'll be back from the little boys' room with another set. If you don't leave me, I'll make the next hour all requests. Just stick it in the bucket."

Another cheer. People loved to hear the songs they chose, and I didn't mind. Most singers hated covers of other people's songs, but they suited me fine. My own songs were more for me than anyone. But the bar owner did mind when he lost customers, so I needed to make it quick, which was never easy with a crowd.

I had made it to the men's room and was almost back, having nearly reached the stage without getting too caught up, when a hand clasped my shoulder from behind.

"Bringing your A-game today, Hudson."

I turned around. "Holy shit."

I reached out my hand to Bruce Allen, owner of the most popular honky-tonk on the street and the first person who'd hired me down here. I still played for him at least every other Sunday, but since his divorce and taking on a co-owner, I hadn't actually seen him for nearly two months.

"Sorry I've been MIA. Sundays are my day with the kids," Bruce said.

"No problem. It's just good to see you."

"You're sounding fantastic."

"Thanks," I said. "And I should probably get back up there." An empty stage was a death knell on Broadway since there was always another bar with music, usually just next door.

"Of course. But listen, I know you're not pushing for a session, but I mentioned your name to a producer friend of mine just last week. Giving you the heads-up in case you hear from a guy named Ray Spencer."

I blinked, trying to figure out if Bruce was serious. "*The* Ray Spencer?"

He smiled. Yeah, he was serious. "That's the one."

"Since when are you friends with Ray Spencer?"

Bruce winked. "Since we share the same divorce attorney. One of these days I'll have to tell you how we met. Crazy story."

Knowing Bruce, I didn't doubt it.

"Thanks, Bruce," I said, slapping him on the shoulder as

he did mine. "I appreciate it. Good to see you. I'll stop in on a day off."

"In between all your jobs?" he called out as I walked to the stage. I lifted my arm and gave him a thumbs-up. He always had a good time with my alter ego. Even threatened to show up at Encore one night, though thankfully he never had.

Avoiding eye contact with more women than I could count, knowing I had to get back onstage, I jumped up onto it amidst another round of cheers. Picking up my guitar and then the tip bucket, I pulled out a slip.

The crowd would like this one. "'Wagon Wheel,'" I said into the microphone before pushing the stool I'd used for the last song to the side. "I'd say 'drinks up,' but I don't have one."

I'd had no chance to stop at the bar, but that wouldn't be a problem. As I retuned my guitar, two whiskeys were brought up to the stage by my regulars. I thanked them both and lifted one into the air.

"Drinks up."

The woman from last night was looking at me.

I made eye contact, nodded, and took a drink as she did the same. She wasn't wearing her sash today. As I started singing, the crowd along with me, I kept glancing back inadvertently. I noticed she sang every word. Country music fan?

god help me, I didn't want anything to do with an engaged woman, or even a customer for that matter, though I might have made an exception in her case for the latter.

Three songs, and two whiskeys later, I stopped for a quick break. My phone had buzzed in my back pocket during the last song, so I pulled it out to check it quickly. It was a number I didn't recognize.

Hi Hudson. My name is Dominica, from Kitchi Falls. Your aunt Dorothy gave me your number. Hope it's ok to shoot you a quick question?

What the hell?

I sent a quick text back.

Sure thing

Curious, I stalled for a time by heading to the request bin, taking out a slip. And since I was a glutton for punishment, I sought out the beautiful bride once again, glancing at the bar. She was on her phone. A second later, she looked up as my own phone buzzed.

My friends and I are in Nashville for a bachelorette party. Dorothy told me that you dance down here.

I knew for a fact my aunt was mortified by my second gig, so it was shocking she'd told her. Also, she said "down here" as if they were here now.

"You really like your sing-alongs," I told the crowd. "Anyone know the words to 'Somethin' 'Bout a Truck?'"

As the crowd clapped, I fired off another text.

U here now?

I was about ready to put my phone away when I looked at her. She glanced down, as if she had just gotten a text.

No fucking way. It couldn't be her. What were the odds?

On a whim, I turned to the crowd and said, "Which one of you is texting me for a date?"

They laughed long enough to give me time to read her response.

We are. And I have a HUGE favor to ask. My sister-in-law is getting married. We took her to a male revue last night, but she had to leave early. We were hoping to make it up to her, but shows seem to be sold out tonight. Any chance you could help us out?

Could this possibly be the same group Dominica was talking about? I scanned the group of friends from the VIP table last night to find the two unfamiliar faces. Could one of them be the friend who "had to leave early"? Wait, not just *a friend* who had to leave early. But her sister-in-law who was getting married.

I watched the woman from last night looking periodically at her phone while talking to her friends. Was this really the same woman texting me right now? Dominica? Was she not actually the bride? The crowd was going to get rowdy any second, but I had to know.

How many women are in your group? How many are getting married?

It was a strange question, but as she looked back down at her phone, I held my breath. Sure enough, she looked around to the others, as if counting, and then started typing on her phone.

Seven. One bride.

It was her.

But I had to get back to my set. I texted her, saying that I'd get back to her ASAP and reluctantly put my phone away. As I did, searching the women a little harder now that I knew what to look for, I noticed one of the women who was not at the table was wearing an off-the-shoulder white sweater. Which reminded me of the white sash.

Holy shit.

She must have been wearing the sash for the exact reason the other guys and I gave her more attention, because she was the "the bride."

Turn around, Dominica, I willed her. As I started to sing, she either heard my silent plea or the universe had plans for us, because she did turn and faced me head-on. Thank god for good eyesight.

No ring.

Game on.

CHAPTER SEVEN

min

"HE TOTALLY JUST LOOKED AT YOU."

Brooke nudged me in the ribs, as if I wasn't already staring at the stage. At first, I'd thought it was my imagination, but he really was. His voice now reminded me of when he whispered in my ear. It was gravelly and low, like that of Stephen Amell's Arrow. I smiled trying to imagine him saying, *You failed this city*.

"Look at that smile," Leeta teased me.

"He's so good," Jen crooned.

"And even better with his clothes off," Amy said. "So sorry you guys missed it," she said to Brooke and Leeta.

"I'm just sorry Brooke didn't get the royal bride treatment," Jen said. "But at least we're feeling better today."

Thayle and I exchanged a conspiratorial glance. During the music break the two of us had been talking about Brooke having gotten off easy when she and Leeta left. Which was when I remembered Dorothy's nephew. I'd texted him, asking for help, and now I waited to hear back. It was a total long shot, but if he could hook us up . . .

"Um, Min?" Thayle waved her hand in front of my face

to get my attention. And I wasn't even drinking at the moment. After two days of hard partying, I was taking advantage of the big orange water coolers in the corners of every bar. Gotta hydrate when day drinking.

"She needs another drink." Leeta proceeded to order me a Deep Eddy and soda while I pretended to be coy, looking away for at least five seconds before turning my attention back to the stage.

"I can't decide if he's sexier today or last night," Amy said.

Definitely today. He was back on the stool, one leg on the ground and the other one propped on the stool's rung. There was just something about a guy who could play music. And that voice . . .

"He's amazing. I wonder why he hasn't struck it big?"

"Everyone down here is that good. Must be hard to stand out."

I half heard the conversation behind me as he sang to me. There was no doubt in my mind now. He may have been in a room full of women fawning over him nearly as hard as they were last night, but Mateo, if that was his real name, was one hundred percent singing to me. His gaze never left me.

The song ended.

"Min, he just winked at you."

Indeed, he did.

"Well, folks, you know what they say about all good things."

A collective groan was accompanied by the sexy singer taking off his guitar. Trying to avoid being so obvious, I turned back to my group.

"Did you or did you not say your goal was to kiss a cowboy this weekend?" Amy asked.

I laughed. "What gives you the impression he's a cowboy?"

"He's as much a cowboy as you're likely to find in Nashville. Or were you thinking to kiss a real one?" Thayle looked around. "Nope. No cattle. Just as I thought."

"Does it matter? Look at that guy," Tina said. "And you should see him without clothes," she told Brooke and Leeta.

"Unfortunately, it looks like, cowboy or not, you're not going to get a chance to kiss him." Thayle nodded to the door.

"Where did he go?" I'd only been turned around for like two minutes. Yet there was no sign of him. A new band was already onstage setting up. I looked around the bar. Nothing.

"Well, that sucks. He was definitely eyeing you up." Brooke waved down the bartender. "Can we get a round of shots?"

Everyone started protesting at once. "We should be buying you shots, not the other way around."

As Brooke explained that she wanted to thank everyone for being here this weekend with a toast, I continued to scan the bar. So much for the wink. My singer/stripper was gone.

As shots were poured, I pulled out my phone, which had buzzed with a text.

Sorry about that. I'm off tonight. Want me to bring a friend over for a private?

What the hell did that mean?

"Thayle," I whispered, since this was supposed to be a surprise for Brooke. "What is this?"

She took my phone and read it. "Private show, I think." She typed something.

"What are you doing?" I asked Thayle, my best friend

since kindergarten. She was probably the only person in the world I'd hand over my phone to and allow to text as me, no questions asked.

"Saying yes."

"Okay, ladies," Brooke said, handing out shot glasses.

"Just so you know," the bartender said, "the shot's called a woo woo. You have to finish it with a 'woo woo' loud enough for the whole bar to hear."

Just a gimmick to infuse a vibe, but I was here for it anyway, despite the fact that Dream Man ditched the bar so quickly.

"Got it," Brooke said, lifting her shot glass. "Here's to no more hangovers, an incredible weekend in Nashville, and the best friends and future family a girl can ask for."

We all downed our shots and promptly yelled, "Woo woo," which got us a whole lot of cheers from the bar. I really did love this place, even if there wouldn't be any cowboy kisses.

"Oooh, he texted back," Thayle said. I looked over her shoulder as she started typing already, but I couldn't read the text.

"What did he say?"

"He told me the cost and asked for a time and address."

"I'll pay, whatever it is. I just really hope he's not some kind of serial killer."

Thayle gave me a look. "We'll all chip in. And you really think Dorothy's nephew might be a serial killer?"

"Okay, probably not," I said. "What time are you thinking? Brooke will wonder why we're going back to the house."

"We'll think of something. I'm asking for seven o'clock. Kind of a pregame before we head back out."

"Pregame," I laughed. "I thought that's what this was." I waved my hand around the bar.

"Yeah, well, I think Brooke's 'no more hangovers' toast was kind of premature," she whispered. "But we'll deal with that later."

"What are you texting now?" I tried to get a look, but Thayle wouldn't let me see. Finally, she handed back my phone just as Jen asked what the two of us were whispering about.

"We'll tell you later," she said as I began to laugh at Thayle's text. Hudson had asked if we had a costume request. Her response?

Cowboy please 🤠

One final scan of the bar confirmed that my singer was gone for good. He had not stuck around to talk to me. Apparently there had been nothing between us, as I'd imagined. When he'd looked at me with those dreamy eyes while he sang, he'd just been doing his job, just like last night—working the crowd, nothing more. Too bad. The guy was really freaking hot. Too much so, honestly. A guy like that spelled trouble. Lots of girls looking for a one-night stand. He was the exact kind of guy who would run screaming when he found out I was a virgin. Not that I was saving it for marriage, but my brothers had sufficiently scared me into being extra cautious when I was younger. Marco had always been the bluntest. With my first serious boyfriend, senior year in high school, he'd said, "Not for anything, Min, but your first time will suck unless the guy really knows what he's doing. And at this age, he doesn't. You're better off waiting until you meet someone who can do it right."

So I had waited. And waited, and waited, until now I'd waited so long that no one seemed to fit the bill. It had made my brothers inordinately happy, me being a virgin, until they'd teased me so bad one night two years ago that I'd blurted out the truth of the matter. "Just because I haven't had sex doesn't mean I haven't had a good time with men. Assholes."

"You like that?" Thayle asked.

She thought I was laughing about the text. "I do. But I was actually thinking about the time I told my brothers I 'had a good time with men' when they were teasing me about being a virgin."

That immediately elicited a laugh from my friend. She'd been there for the fireworks. "Literally one of my favorite memories."

Between my brothers pretending to be gagging and asking for names, playing the part of macho older brothers perfectly, the lot of them had acted like a gaggle of fools. And yet, I loved all three of them so much, and still couldn't believe Thayle and Neo had gotten together after secretly crushing on each other for years.

"Mine too," I admitted. "Speaking of memories, we'll have to figure out how to get Brooke back to the house in a bit." To that end, it was time to quietly spread the word to the others about our change of plans.

With any luck, Dorothy's nephew would come through and be a half-decent replacement for Brooke. True, she'd been rather thankful to have avoided being "targeted," as she'd called it last night, but we weren't about to let her get off that easy. There would be no hiding in our house tonight.

My future sister-in-law was going to kill me, but it would be totally worth it.

I hoped.

CHAPTER EIGHT

hudson

"You ready?"

Oliver shot me a look, pausing with his hand midair, on the verge of knocking on the door. "I don't know how you roped me into this."

I looked him up and down. "No pun intended?"

He shook his head. "One Saturday night off all month."

"Look at it this way. You can earn a few bucks and still go out later. Win-win."

"You're coming with me."

"Oh no, I've had my fill for the day. I'm beat."

Oliver lowered his hand. "You're either working or home reading one of those goddamned books of yours. I thought I made being my wingman a stipulation of this gig."

"First of all, those damn books of mine are how I know I'm better off going home than getting into more trouble with you later." That was what I got for admitting my addiction to self-help books. So I had an obsession with getting to know myself better. Being a better person. Turned out, the guys thought it wasn't so much enlightened as it was downright strange. "Second of all, you said no such thing."

"I'm saying it now."

After playing all day, the last thing I felt like doing was heading back out, but Oliver was doing me a solid here. "Fine. But I'm not closing anything down."

His smile said he knew that wouldn't be true. Reaching up, he knocked on the door. I stood behind him, anticipating her reaction. Knowing I'd see her again tonight, I'd skipped out earlier and focused on convincing Ollie to agree to a last-minute private. But now that I was seconds away from seeing her again, the anticipation was killing me.

I'd been around plenty of drop-dead gorgeous women in this profession, not to mention the singing gigs, so it wasn't just that. The woman exuded life. She smiled big, hugged her friends with abandon, and last night, she felt pretty fucking good against me. At the time I hadn't allowed myself to respond. I'd gotten pretty good at separating myself from the job, all the easier when I'd thought she was engaged.

But tonight?

Fraternizing with clients was one of those no-nos that most of the guys ignored with a few exceptions. Dominic, because he was married. Me, mostly, because one-night stands had begun to feel hollow years ago. If I was being honest, though, since this afternoon I'd thought more than once about kissing Miss Dominica from Kitchi Falls. When I'd begged Ollie to come, I'd told him she was from my hometown, which was basically true. Kitchi Falls was less than twenty minutes from Brookville, located on the other side of the lake. My parents met in Kitchi Falls when Mom did a training at the school where my dad was the principal. When I was five, he got a job across the lake in

Brookville as a superintendent, but we visited Kitchi Falls periodically since most of his family still lived there.

Dominica's friend opened the door.

"Sorry to interrupt," Oliver said. "We heard there were some fillies in the area that might need to be tamed."

I rolled my eyes. That opener had to be one of the worst of them.

Nevertheless, the pretty blonde smiled. "As a matter of fact . . ."

She opened the door wide and stepped aside. The same ladies from earlier were all there. Except her.

As one of the veteran dancers at Encore, Oliver knew what he was doing. He strolled into the living room and turned on his Bluetooth speakers before they all sat down. "Is it true one of you is getting married next month?"

Good news, they pointed at the real bride of the group.

Bad news, Dominica was nowhere to be found. As the ladies squealed when Oliver made a beeline for the bride, I scanned the house. Nothing.

"I make one phone call all day—"

She stopped short, coming from around the corner. The look on her face was everything I'd hoped it would be. She stared at me, and then Oliver. That was when I noticed she wasn't the only one. At least a few of the ladies sensed the sparks flying between us. But it took them a lot less time to get used to the idea. Pretty quickly they were focused on Oliver, who'd tipped his hat to the bride and was already taking off his clothes piece by piece in front of her.

I played my part too, leaning against the wall chewing on a piece of straw. Trying my best to look bored, I watched her sit on the couch, still staring at me.

She pulled out her phone. It didn't take long for mine to vibrate.

Seriously?

Placing my phone on the fireplace mantel next to me, I winked at her in response as I'd done earlier that day. She didn't smile, exactly, but there was no doubt Dominica looked at me the same way I was looking at her. And then her friend grabbed and shook her shoulder.

She turned to see Oliver now wearing only boots, a thong and a cowboy hat, giving the bride a lap dance to a sensual country song. Dominica laughed and then lifted her phone up to take a picture.

Every one of the women was smiling. And my mom wanted me to use my education degree, and follow in her and Dad's footsteps? Spending my life in a classroom being told to give students standardized tests? Fuck that. It hadn't taken me many ed courses in college to realize I'd made a huge mistake, that the current education system so devalued creativity I would never last.

They might be embarrassed by me, my father especially, but I wasn't. Not in the slightest.

Oliver jumped off the bride's lap as the song came to an end. "That was what we call a Nashville welcome," he said. "What's your name, bride-to-be?"

"Brooke," she said.

"Well, Brooke, your friends were sorry you missed our show the other night so—" He waved his arm to me. "I brought the most popular cowboy in town to you."

A new song started up. But instead of moving toward the group, I continued my hard-to-get routine and remained leaning against the wall.

Oliver grabbed his discarded clothes and tossed them to the side. "Hudson? What do you say?"

The ladies cheered, but there was only one I watched. "I'm gonna need a chair."

One of the women jumped up and headed to the kitchen. When she brought a chair back, I nodded to the center of the room Oliver had so nicely cleared. Since he'd just given Brooke a lap dance, I didn't feel badly about crooking my finger to Dominica instead, telling her to "come here."

Of course a woman like her would bristle at such a high-handed command. I'd have expected nothing less. But I also knew she wanted to come. Working hard not to smile as we stared each other down, it was only when her friends pushed her off the couch, yelling, "Come on, Min," that she finally did get up.

"In the seat," I commanded. Her eyes narrowed, but she complied, sliding into the seat. Now that she was thoroughly annoyed with me, it was time to turn that frown upside down.

CHAPTER NINE
dominica

I STILL COULDN'T BELIEVE IT.

As Hudson—aka Mateo, aka hot singer—finally pushed away from the wall and made his way toward us, I alternately stared in fascination and tried to get Thayle to stop making kissy faces. I wasn't sure which one of them I wanted to kill first.

The music changed, another slow country song, but he didn't come near me. Instead, Hudson began to dance beside me, giving his complete attention to Brooke. He wore jeans with chaps and a vest, but his arms and abs were already fully on display. Sure, it was his job to look good, but that level of muscle had to come with a price. He probably ate protein powder for a snack and avoided alcohol like the plague. I dated a guy who was seriously into bodybuilding, and while I'd admired his commitment, it was kind of a drag too.

Something that was not a drag?

Watching this guy move. I began to come out of my shock from seeing him, from thinking back to this afternoon at the bar and realizing he had known, somehow, he'd been texting me. When he'd winked at me from the stage, he had known he'd be coming here tonight.

He moved from Brooke to each of the girls, his hips circling in ways I didn't even know were possible. And then he turned to me. At this point, his chaps were gone but he still wore jeans. Correction. Those were coming off too. First, he removed his belt and then everyone in the room screamed as he tore off the jeans. When he danced behind me, I knew instinctively what he was going to do . . . again.

Sure enough, with my hands now pulled behind the chair, he used the belt to tie them together. Then leaning down to me, he whispered, "You seemed to like it last night."

Ohmygod. Ohmygod. Ohmygod.

Every move he made was sexier than the one before it. When he dropped to all fours, his hands splayed on my thighs, and began to grind, his face way closer to my crotch than anyone had been in a long time, the girls went nuts.

His ass cheeks hardly moved. Even they were toned to perfection. By the time Hudson had jumped back up and torn off his vest, the urge to touch him had grown so strong I actually strained against the belt. Then, as suddenly as it started, the song stopped. He moved behind me, untied my hands, and then began to pick up his clothes. I tried to stand, but my legs were a bit wobbly, so I sat back down for a second. Another song had started, and his friend began to dance, this time giving Tina his full attention.

Trying again, I was successful on my second attempt to stand. Sitting back down on the couch, I spent the rest of the forty-five minutes alternately pretending not to have been affected by Hudson and, when he wasn't looking, stealing peeks at him.

"I don't know how you guys pulled this off," Brooke

said when the last song ended. Hudson and his friend were getting dressed, a sad moment indeed.

"It was Min's idea," Thayle said. "He's Dorothy's nephew."

Brooke's jaw dropped. "What?" She said to Hudson, "Dorothy Williams is your aunt?"

All eyes turned to Hudson, who was now, unfortunately, fully dressed.

"She is. You ladies all from Kitchi Falls?"

While everyone told him where they were from, I watched him, though Hudson made no effort to look at me. It was a show. Last night, this afternoon, just now. This guy was a performer, and if he made it seem like he was singling me out in the crowd, that was all it was. An act.

"Brooke didn't feel well last night—"

"Don't sugarcoat it," Leeta said. "Both of us had massive hangovers that we couldn't shake. This city is a killer."

"Only if you overindulge," Oliver said. "Which is what you're here for, so," he shrugged, "comes with the territory."

"I suppose," Brooke conceded. "But I'm almost glad we're only here two more days. Not sure I'd last much longer."

"Two days?" Oliver asked. "What have you done so far? I'll make sure you don't miss anything good." Tina and Brooke rattled off the places we'd been so far. "So all of Broadway? Have you been to Printer's Alley yet?"

"We were heading there tonight," Tina said, "until Min hired you guys."

Both Hudson and Oliver looked at me. Hudson hadn't said anything yet, and it didn't seem like he would. His friend was much more of a talker.

"There's still time." Oliver picked up his phone and speaker. They were leaving. "Saturday is a good night down there. You might like the burlesque show at Skull's."

"We heard about that," Thayle said. "But apparently there's a line around the block. They say it's impossible to get in on a Saturday night."

"You guys are still up for a night on the town, right?" Amy asked the other girls. Everyone agreed they were. They thanked Oliver and Hudson and began to move, getting up from their seats and prepping for a night out.

"We can get you in." Hudson had spoken to me.

I'd heard his voice before, two nights in a row when he'd whispered into my ear. And today when he sang and talked to the crowd. But this was his regular voice, and I liked it. Low and gravelly, and as sexy as the man himself.

"We don't want to put you out," Brooke began, clearly not picking up on the dynamics here. Thayle's not-so-subtle swat on the arm basically told her to zip it.

"You're planning to go there too?" I asked. If he was going to get us in and leave, I wanted to be prepared for it. That way I could tell my rapidly beating heart that I'd been right all along, that he had no interest in me, and he was just being nice by getting us into a club.

"We were heading somewhere." Hudson turned to his friend. "You don't care where we go?"

"Nah, man, fine with me. They've seen enough of these bodies these past two nights. Let's go look at some real beauty."

Everyone laughed except us. Hudson and I continued to look at one another, an understanding passing between us. He wasn't just dropping us off at Skull's, he was coming with us. If my legs had been wobbly before, they were positively useless now. I didn't even try to use them.

"Mind if we use your bedrooms to change, if we're heading right there?" Oliver asked, waving down at his outfit.

We greeted him with a "no problem" and "you can use the two at the end of the hall" chorus; the idea of Oliver and Hudson . . . the idea of Oliver and Hudson changing in our bedrooms as appealing to the others as it was to me.

"Great," Hudson said. "We'll be quick."

They went to the bathroom door, Tina thankfully being the one to show them the way. I had yet to move. The minute the guys went into their respective bedrooms, the girls went nuts.

"Skull's Rainbow Room in Printer's Alley," Amy said, "in Nashville, escorted by two male entertainers. Are you serious right now?"

"Best bachelorette party weekend ever," Tina declared.

Thayle was looking at me. "I have a feeling," she said, smiling, "Min will get her chance to kiss a cowboy after all. He was all over you."

I rolled my eyes. "That's his job, Thayle. The other guy was all over Brooke, and the rest of you."

A round of protests rose up as all of the girls agreed it wasn't the same, that Hudson was into me. Maybe they were right. And it would be a good thing, because I was really, really into him too.

CHAPTER TEN

"What are you ladies doing back here?" Oliver asked as we approached them.

The women were standing in line around the corner, far enough from the entrance that they'd have no chance of getting into the show.

Oliver said, "Come on."

She was at the front of the pack. Not surprising, as Dominica—or Min, as her friends called her—seemed to be in charge of the weekend. At their house, just before we left, the bride had asked her what they had planned for the next day.

When we reached the front entrance, Sam, the bouncer, looked at Oliver and me like he was about to kill us. Sliding the two of us inside, no problem. A group this big? He was going to catch some flak for it from the people in line. Thankfully he didn't hesitate.

"There you are," he said. "The owner's been waiting on you guys for an hour. Get your asses inside."

Winking at him, I slipped Sam a bill just in time to hear the grumbling behind us. Sure enough, the place was packed. The long stage to the right was empty, but one of the dancers looked like she was just about to start her set. Winding our way through the front room to the bar at the back, we squeezed into a spot.

"What does everyone want?" I asked them.

"You aren't buying for us," the blonde said. "Not after getting us in here. I got this."

My mother raised a gentleman, so I ignored her and went to the bar anyway. Catching the bartender's attention easily enough, as I knew her from around town, I ordered my drink and Oliver's and then caught Dominica's eye. It was as good an excuse as any to talk to her.

"What do you and your friends want to drink?"

Caught between me and the blonde, with me at the bar ready to order, she gave in. After collecting our drink orders, we divvied them up, and I shifted to Dominica's other side, where it was less crowded. Then, tucking myself into a corner, pleased she understood and came over, we stood together, drinks in hand. I knew already from dancing with her, but the woman smelled so fucking good. Like a vanilla cupcake. Sweet, but with a hint of spice too.

"Thanks for the drink," she said. "You didn't have to do that. I should be buying yours for coming to the house tonight on such late notice."

"No problem. I'm glad I was free. Your friend seemed to have a good time."

"You caught that?" She didn't hold back her smile. If it wasn't so trite sounding, I'd have told her she had the nicest smile, because she did. "She's marrying my brother next month."

"February in Kitchi Falls? She likes to play chicken with Mother Nature?"

Her laugh in response slayed me. The music had started, but neither of us were looking at the stage.

"Long story, but basically my brothers and I own a winery."

"Say no more. I grew up in Brookville and am pretty familiar with the wine industry. Which winery?"

"Grado Valley Vineyards."

"No shit? I've been there a few times. Grado's a legend on Seneca Lake."

"My parents planted the first vines over thirty years ago. They just retired last year and left my brothers and me the whole thing."

"That must be exciting. But scary too."

"Exactly. No one wants to screw up something their parents built and cultivated their whole lives. My brother Cosimo is proprietor and feels the most pressure, I think."

"The one getting married?"

She looked at Brooke. Her friends were all not-so-subtly watching us. "Yep, that's the one. By the way, that was a nice stunt you pulled, calling me out onstage. Shocked the hell out of me."

I wondered when she'd get around to that. "You liked that?"

She scrunched her nose. Adorable. "I'm not one hundred percent certain. I like surprises, but that definitely threw me. How did you figure out the person texting you was in the audience?"

Never one for subtleties, I gave her the truth. "I'd been watching you during my set and just put two and two together. The night before I saw two of the ladies in your group leave. And you mentioned the bride left early the night before, so . . ." I took a swig of beer.

"You saw them leave?"

More truth bombs. "I took notice of you with your friends last night too, even before I came to your table."

Not surprisingly, the air between us shifted from innocent to something more. Dominica looked into my eyes and hopefully saw my admiration there. Blinking, she looked away, toward the stage.

"Oh my god," she said. "She's taking her clothes off."

Reluctantly I turned from my companion to the stage. "Indeed she is. That's Molly. She's been here the longest of any of the women. I take it you've never been to a burlesque show?"

Dominica shook her head. "Nope. They aren't exactly popular in Kitchi Falls. I have traveled a bit, but. . ." she shrugged, ". . . no. I didn't know exactly what it was, to be honest. She's so beautiful."

Molly was a very pretty woman, and she knew how to work a crowd. But I was looking at someone even more beautiful, though I didn't mention it. She'd think I was a super-stalker.

"Those moves," I said instead, "are her signature ones. She teaches belly dancing classes too. Most of the women here don't do this full time."

"Like you?" she asked.

"Exactly."

"It's hard to believe singing doesn't pay the bills. You're incredible."

Getting compliments almost daily about my singing, my dancing, and other less noteworthy things like the state of my muscles, I didn't usually think much of them. But coming from her . . .

"Thanks, but no, it doesn't. Probably could, but I like variety."

"Hmm," she said, "I bet."

"I meant in my profession. Not in women."

She raised her brows. "You're telling me a man who looks like you, and sings and moves like you do, doesn't have his pick of groupies every night?"

The slow, sensual music of the song coupled with the red and black interior, and now a second drink shoved into my hand courtesy of Oliver, contributed to the left turn of our discussion.

"Groupies?" I said. She might be smiling, but her question was a serious one. Which meant it was a good time to clear the air. "First of all, I don't have groupies. Second of all, the answer is no. I'm a one-woman kind of guy."

Her immediate show of skepticism was not a surprise. "I don't believe you."

"I can tell."

"Min," another of the women said, sidling up to her. "Sorry to butt in, but do you need another drink?"

"I'm good for now," she said, "thanks."

"Min. Short for Dominica?"

"Yep. One of my brothers started calling me that when we were young and it stuck."

"The one getting married?"

"Nope. The one most likely never to get married. Marco. Our third brother, Antonio, is engaged to her." She nodded to her friend who'd just asked about a drink. "Thayle's been my best friend since kindergarten."

"Your brother is marrying your best friend?"

Dominica beamed. "Yep. It's the best. Apparently, they had a crush on each other forever, but no one suspected."

"Not even you?"

She shook her head. "Nope. I feel like an idiot now, but I was clueless. I mean, I knew she thought he was cute, but that was back in middle school. I assumed she had grown out of it."

"So you have three brothers. Any sisters?"

"No. You?"

"None. I wish. So are you the oldest? Middle child?"

"I'm the youngest."

"Let me guess. Twenty-four?"

"Twenty-five. You?"

"The ripe old age of twenty-nine."

"Ouch," I teased. "So, your aunt said you actually spent some time with her a few years back?"

Beautiful. Outgoing. Easy to talk to. Talk about a trifecta. How was she not already taken? No ring didn't mean no boyfriend, but the vibe I was getting was unattached.

"I did. Although I was too young to hit the wineries back then, at only twelve. Though I have been to Grado twice with friends, once when I still lived at home and then two summers ago on a visit."

"I was working there full time two years ago, but you probably were in the Wine Cellar. The big tasting room."

"Big deck on the back?"

"Yep, that's the main room. I'm in charge of the Wine Barn, a separate winery on-site."

"I do remember the place was huge."

"We add on all the time. But the Barn is my favorite. It was modeled to look like a repurposed Tuscan barn. With wine."

"Sounds like a pretty sweet place to work."

"Sure is," she said. "But maybe not as sweet as onstage singing to adoring fans. Or—" She stopped.

"Or being groped by a bunch of strange women?"

She appeared thoughtful. "You don't like that part of the job?"

"It's just that, a job. Having someone run their hands across my abs is probably the same as you pouring a glass of wine for a customer."

She responded with an infectious laugh. "I hardly would count the two as the same."

I could tell she wanted to ask me something. "Ask away. Any question is fair game."

She looked at the stage and then back to me. "Any question?"

"Yep. Anything."

So it was possible to embarrass Dominica Grado. Interesting. Everything about her screamed uninhibited, but there was no mistaking that she was unsure about whatever she was planning to ask.

I closed some of the distance between us and lowered my voice. "Ask," I said, taking a swig of beer. After darting a glance over to Oliver, who was holding court with the rest of Dominica's friends, I looked back to my companion.

"Do you ever . . ." Again, the nose scrunch thing. Her deep brown eyes were so expressive. Seductive too. "You know, when you're dancing. Do you ever . . . *like* a customer?"

"Like?" I considered teasing her but decided not to torture her. "You mean do we ever get erections while dancing?"

"I mean, kind of. Yes, actually."

I wanted to kiss this woman so fucking bad. How she managed to be adorable and sexy all at once, I had no idea. But she did, and it took everything in me not to want to feel her against me again, but this time, with fewer prying eyes.

"Sometimes, yes," I said. "And to answer your next question, yes. I got one today dancing for you."

She blinked. Did I go too far?

Before she could respond, one of her friends approached us. "So did you tell him yet?"

"Tell him what?" Dominica asked as the music and conversation flowed all around us.

"That your goal this weekend was to kiss a cowboy?"

I nearly spat out my drink. Thankfully I managed to get it down without completely embarrassing myself.

"You are a dead woman, Leeta," Dominica said.

Leeta didn't seem too worried. "Just thought I'd ask. Sorry to interrupt. I'll grab you a drink to make it up to you."

Sure enough, we watched as Leeta rejoined the others. It seemed that had been a joint effort, as the entire group, Oliver included, watched us.

"So you want to kiss a cowboy this weekend?"

"I am so sorry. They're just busting my chops. I know there aren't actual cowboys here. It was just a joke, you know, the whole jeans-and-cowboy-hat vibe." She shook her head. "Oh my god, I'm making it worse." She couldn't possibly get any cuter. "Just ignore them. Ignore me, I'm rambling now."

"Ignore you? I don't think that's possible." I took her vodka and put it, along with my beer, on a high-top near us. "But your friends are all looking. I think we should give them a bit of a show, don't you?"

"You mean . . ." She stared at my lips. I wanted her to give me the go-ahead, the anticipation of tasting this woman nearly my undoing.

"I do, Dominica. You have three seconds to tell me no. Otherwise, your Nashville goal is about to be achieved."

One.
She tilted her head up to me.
Two.
Her lips parted.
Three.
I reached for her neck and pulled her toward me.

CHAPTER ELEVEN

dominica

EVERYTHING ABOUT THIS NIGHT WAS JUST . . . SURREAL. TALKING to Hudson was surprisingly easy given that he wasn't really human. Guys like him existed in a separate world, one where mortals didn't exist. Kind of like billionaires on massive yachts. Like some separate reality.

Except, he was talking to me as if he wasn't some sort of Greek god. As if he was one of us. I'd nearly strangled Leeta when she came over here. I had no doubt the group put her up to it. But I couldn't argue with her methods.

You have three seconds to tell me no. Otherwise, your Nashville goal is about to be achieved.

He was seriously going to kiss me. Here, in the middle of this bar. Maybe not exactly the middle. We were tucked away pretty well. But still.

On one, I tried to imagine what kissing him would be like. Though he'd ditched the hat, he still wore jeans, cowboy boots and a flannel.

On two, my heart nearly leapt from my chest in anticipation.

On three, his hand shot out. When he reached behind my neck, I knew this wasn't going to be any old kiss. And it wasn't. The first touch of his lips on mine was so electrifying, my knees nearly buckled. I'd honestly thought that expression was an exaggeration. But literally, if not for his other arm around my back, I might not have continued to stand.

Hudson kissed as good as he looked. His lips moved over mine so effortlessly, his tongue demanding I meet him halfway. Another song began, and I was sure we were being watched, but I didn't care. Nothing mattered but the flex of his arms under my fingertips, the way he drew me in, deeper and deeper. I never wanted this kiss to end.

And then, he made a sound. A deep, guttural man-sound that made me think he liked this kiss as much as I did. When he did pull away, it was like going to the refrigerator, starving, and seeing that your healthy self had done the grocery shopping.

But I couldn't yell "dammit" since there was no fridge door to shut. And stomping my feet in frustration didn't seem like a good idea either.

Although we had stopped kissing, Hudson hadn't moved away. His hand was still splayed on my lower back, and mine rested on his arm. I didn't *want* to move away, and if I was behaving like a petulant child, well then, so be it.

"Goal achieved," I said finally.

Hudson continued to stare into my eyes, and no part of me wanted to look away.

"I have a confession," Hudson said.

"I can only imagine." It definitely had something to do with his claim of being a one-woman man, as if a guy like him didn't have more women than Jimmy Carter had peanuts, as my mom liked to say.

He leaned down, tucked a strand of hair behind my ear and whispered into it, "I'm not really a cowboy."

I wanted to ask Hudson to kiss me there while he was at it, but even I wasn't that forward. So when he stood back up and reached for our drinks, finally moving away (dammit), I said nothing and simply took the drink.

"Well, that's a disappointment." I took a sip of the lemonade-flavored vodka and peeked at the stage. These women really were crazy talented.

The fact that he smiled in response rather than taking it as a slight told me a lot about him. Not that he hadn't exuded confidence from the get-go, but still. Just to make sure he knew I was teasing, I told him, "If I had known I'd get a kiss like that down here, my goal would have been to kiss a stripper-singer instead."

He stared at my lips. I knew what he was feeling and wanted to do it again too. But a quick glance over to the girls told me what I already knew.

"We're being watched," Hudson said.

"By more than just our group," I said, noticing a woman staring at us from the bar for the first time. "Don't look now, but there's a really pretty dark-haired woman, hair pulled up into a pony, at the bar looking at us."

He looked. "Sorry. Reflex. She's an ex," he said.

I rolled my eyes. "Of course she is."

His face fell. It was the first time since we'd met that Hudson looked anything but pleased, or content, or happy. I'd hurt him with those words and immediately wanted to take them back. But before I could, he asked if I wanted another drink.

"I'm good. We started pretty early."

"Alright," he said. "Be right back."

Instead of standing solo, and not wanting to completely abandon my friends, I walked over to the group. They'd split up a bit since the bar was long and narrow without room for such a large group, and Thayle was talking to Oliver. I caught them mid-conversation.

"He's actually Min's brother. We've known each other since I started kindergarten," Thayle said.

"Chatting about my big brother?"

"One of the three," Thayle said, peeking at the stage. It was hard not to look. Everything about this place was cool. The decor, the entertainment, the vibe.

Hudson.

"Three big brothers," Oliver marveled.

"Big Italian brothers," Thayle emphasized. "Which is different from regular big brothers. They can be . . . intense when it comes to Min."

"In other words," the deep voice from behind me said, "they would probably not be thrilled to see your sister making out with a guy who was grinding on her a few hours ago?" Hudson asked, handing Oliver a beer.

He stood next to me, so close I could smell his cologne. Whatever it was, I counted it as my new favorite scent in the world.

"Let me think . . ." Thayle pretended to ponder that one. "I'm gonna go with no. But they will never find out, so all is well."

"Is it ever weird that your fiancée and best friend are siblings?" Oliver asked. "What if he asked outright what she was up to this weekend?"

"First of all," Thayle said. "There is no 'if.' He will definitely ask. Neo has to know everything about everything. Am I right?" she asked me.

I was having a hard time concentrating on the conversation with Hudson so close to me. Getting that kiss out of my brain would not be an easy feat.

"You are." I looked at Hudson. Bad mistake. The bouncer, all the way across the bar, could probably sense how badly I wanted to kiss Hudson again.

"What would they say about you coming to see my set tomorrow? I'm playing second floor at Tootsie's from noon to two."

He wanted to see me again.

After sticking my foot in my mouth earlier, I'd thought for sure I'd blown it.

"Tomorrow? Skipping out already?" Oliver asked him. Hudson looked to me for an answer.

"You ladies calling it an early night?" Hudson asked me, the last show of the night having just ended.

Thayle opened her mouth to speak, but I wasn't going to chance what might come out.

"If you even think about heading back at midnight on our second to last night in Nashville, I will disown you," I said.

"As a friend or sister-in-law?"

"Shit. I keep forgetting. That does make it harder."

Thayle laughed but nodded to the others. "I know Brooke and Jen are up for staying after missing half of last night. Let me check with the others." She gave me a conspiratorial smirk. "But I'm game to stay out for sure."

When Thayle left, Oliver looked between Hudson and me, muttered something about being a proper wingman, and headed in the opposite direction to talk to someone he knew.

"Looks like we're staying out," I said, praying he would too. "Any suggestions on where to hit next?"

"A few, but honestly next door is as good a place as anywhere. There's a cover, but we can get you all in."

"That's the first bar I've seen with a cover down here."

"There's a few of them, especially on Saturday nights. Crowd control. I know the act and they're a great band."

"Sounds like a plan to me."

"And about tomorrow," I said, not wanting to ignore his earlier question. "I'm sure the girls would love to come listen to your set. We tried to get into Tootsie's the day we came, but it was a madhouse."

"The girls?" he asked, the corners of his mouth lifting in a slow, sensual smile. "Or you?"

I loved the fact that he didn't play coy. Unlike his act at the house, Hudson was actually pretty straightforward, which I appreciated. Game playing was one of my least favorite parts of single life.

"Me," I admitted freely.

As a reward for being forthright, I got another smile. This one full of promise. "Good. I have a surprise for you."

"I love surprises," I said, unable to imagine what he might be talking about.

"I know. And I think this one will be right up your alley."

"Speaking of alleys," Oliver said, coming back, this time with Brooke at his side. "The gang's all ready to head into that one." He nodded toward the door. "You kids ready?"

Hudson took my empty glass and put it, along with his bottle, on the bar. Then, as if we hadn't only known each other for a few hours, he took my hand. His fingers wrapped around mine perfectly, his grip as tight as I'd expect from a specimen like him.

"Let's go," he said. When Hudson turned toward Oliver, who was already walking away, I caught Thayle's eye. She pretended to fan herself as if overheating.

"Right?" I mouthed. He was so smoking hot. Now it was just a matter of not getting burned.

CHAPTER TWELVE

hudson

I TRIED TO SING, TO INFUSE THE CROWD WITH AS MUCH SUNDAY Funday vibes as I could muster, but as I waited for Min and her friends, it was becoming harder and harder to concentrate. I could think of exactly zero times in my life when I more greatly anticipated being with a woman.

Even Oliver had said much of the same last night. After two more hours of drinking, singing, and dancing, we closed down the place. I'd give them credit, even though they took an early evening break, those ladies had partied hard all day and night.

Heading out of the bar had been like walking a plank. Even worse, it took us so long to make our way outside, the ladies' Lyfts had already been there awhile waiting, and had been on the verge of leaving without them.

I'd come close to kissing Min again—she said to call her that, as only her parents called her Dominica when she was in trouble—but it was too rushed. The others had been getting into the cars, their drivers impatient to get away from the throng of other bar-goers heading home, and the last thing I'd wanted was another rushed, public kiss. Today I was determined to find a minute alone with her.

After refraining from texting her when I woke up, I packed my bag for a long day and night. After Tootsie's I'd be grabbing a quick bite and heading right to Whiskey Soul, where Encore would be waiting for me. I wanted to spend Min's last night in Nashville doing a show no more than I wanted the whiskey one of my regulars just handed me. Besides, Min was here to have a good time with her friends and sister-in-law. I supposed it was for the best that I was busy. The last thing I wanted to do was get in the way of their girls' trip.

Except, I did want that. I wanted to see her every minute until she left. It was impossible not to smile around her. Min was an invigorating, boundless source of energy and life. Women as attractive as her usually knew it and acted accordingly. If anything, she was just the opposite, her self-deprecation was without a doubt a shield. A way to avoid being hurt. I wanted to know what had hurt her in the past, and what she planned to do this month, next month, and the rest of her life.

I wanted to be a part of it.

"Thank you, folks, glad you enjoyed that one. So who's having a good time so far here in Nashville?" A round of hollers greeted me. "Anyone in the mood for an original?"

Humoring me, the crowd clapped in approval even though what they only ever really wanted were covers. But I'd been working on a new song and wanted to give it a test drive.

As soon as I sat down, she walked in. Leading the pack, she wore a long, open maroon sweater, the edges frayed. Tan cowboy boots and a white tee, her hair down in waves today (it had been straight before) completed the look.

But it was more than she wore or how she styled her hair that set Min apart. It was the way she walked into the room, as if daring anyone to screw with her plans. She was here to have a good time, and no one would get in her way.

"It's called 'Midnight and Promises.'"

I couldn't hide my smile at her expression. She'd stopped, stared, and was now laughing at my outfit.

I hadn't held back. From my boots to the hat, blue button-down and the largest belt buckle I could find, I had leaned into the cowboy role today. And by the look on Min's face, it had been worth the effort.

"Afternoon, ladies," I said into the microphone. "You're just in time for a song. Hope you like country."

Singing with more heart than I had before she arrived, I watched the girls grab drinks and seek out a spot to stand. Settling not far from the stage, crowded around a high-top, they clinked glasses, some of them watching me.

One of them not hiding her appreciation.

"Another night of promises, but none that you keep," I sang, watching her.

When the song was over, she came up to the edge of the front of the stage. "Do you take requests?"

"From you? Always," I said.

"I'm not sure if you know this one," she said, the sparkle in her eyes a warning.

"Try me."

"It's called, 'Kiss a Cowboy.' Ever heard of it?"

Fuck. If I could have jumped off the stage and given this entire place a show without getting fired, I'd have done it in a heartbeat. Maybe it wouldn't have been such a bad thing. Singing had lost some of the joy it brought me before I started doing it full time. But I did need money, so the kiss would have to wait.

"I don't know it," I said. "Maybe you can show me . . . the lyrics? After my set?"

"Happy to," she said, smiling, "cowboy."

With that, Min rejoined her friends while I spent the next hour attempting to recover. By the time my set was done, I was itching with impatience. I strapped my guitar to my back and headed directly to the bartender.

"Hey, Jack," I said.

"Great set, Hudson. I see you have some fans." He nodded to a group of women—not my group but another bachelorette party—all staring at me.

"Thanks." I ignored the part about having fans. "Any chance you have the key for the third-floor storage room?"

"I do. Need to store your stuff?"

"No. I need to say goodbye to someone who's leaving in the morning." I wouldn't be finished with Encore until well after Min and her friends would be hitting the sack. They'd said as much last night, that with a seven a.m. flight, they'd be taking it easy today. Which meant this was it for us.

"No one ever accused me of cockblocking." He handed me the keys. "Here you go."

"Thanks." I took them and made a beeline for the group. "Afternoon, ladies."

"Hudson," Thayle said. "Holy crap, that was so good. You wrote that one song?"

"Yup." I didn't want to be rude, but the urge to pull Min away was strong.

"I still don't know how you aren't super famous," Jen said. "Someday we'll be watching you in a huge arena. I just know it."

"I'm not sure I want that," I said, sneaking a peek at Min.

"Really?" Leeta seemed genuinely surprised.

"Yeah. I thought so—that's why I came down here in the first place. But now," I shrugged. "I don't know." At least a minute had passed, enough that I did not appear completely rude pulling Min aside. "Can I talk to you for a sec?"

As good times rolled around us, Min's friends showed no sign of letting up despite their claims the night before. I'd honestly never met a group of women who could party that hard so many days in a row.

"Sure," she said.

Knowing she wouldn't be needing it, I took her drink from her and handed it to Brooke. "You might as well finish that."

Brooke's jaw dropped.

Although I'd taken Min by the hand last night when we left Skull's and again later that night when we made our way to the bar together, doing it now seemed different. More . . . intimate . . . in the light of day. But she didn't protest. And frankly, it just felt right.

Weaving our way to the third floor, where a bluegrass band was playing, I guided her to the back and unlocked the storage room door. It was dark. But I didn't turn on the light. Instead, I pulled us both inside, laid my guitar against the wall and shut the door, locking it. Grabbing both of Min's hands, I pinned them above her head as she backed up to the door. It was dark, so I couldn't see her face clearly.

I whispered into Min's ear, her body pressed to mine, "You have something to show me?"

Her head leaned back, giving me better access.

"Kiss a Cowboy," Min murmured. Her breath was uneven, her hair now pushed back behind her shoulder.

I planted on kiss behind her ear. And then a second on her neck. The third and fourth, lower each time.

"I think you lied," she said. "I think you do know that song."

"I do."

I claimed her lips and allowed her hands to wrench free. They wrapped immediately around my neck, making lifting her easy. With Min's legs clenched around my waist, my tongue found hers. Slanting my head for better access, I drew out the moment, thankful she was pressed so close to me.

But I wanted her even closer.

Grasping a fistful of her hair in one hand, using the other to keep her propped up, I pulled her in even closer, the kiss so wildly uninhibited I'd have been scared, if not for the certainty that this was the beginning of something, not the end. Deeper and deeper I drew her in, Min accepting every caress.

Releasing her hair, I wrapped my arms around her, wanting to get closer.

The wild abandon she walked into a room with, smiled and danced with, was now directed completely at me. My heart raced like that of an errant schoolboy who had just claimed his first kiss. It was as novel as it was seductive, kissing Dominica Grado. I wanted so very much more.

When the door was wrenched open, light flooding inside, I was too slow releasing her.

"Ah shit, sorry about that, Hudson," the bar's assistant manager said. "Came in for some bar straws."

Bar straws. I would hate those little fuckers forever now.

Min jumped away from me. I reluctantly let her go.

"Don't be sorry for using your own storage room." I could tell Min was embarrassed about having been caught.

"I'll just grab this bad boy"—I picked up my guitar—"and we'll be out of your way."

He chuckled as the two of us ducked back out.

"Oh my god, I nearly died," she said as we made our way from the storeroom back into the bar area up here on the third floor.

"When the door opened?" I led us toward an empty high-top, unwilling to relinquish her to her friends just yet. "Or at the first touch of our lips?"

She laughed, seeming to understand, and took a seat on a stool. "Of course I was talking about the kiss."

After taking off the guitar once again, I leaned it against my stool and said, "Be right back."

This third floor was nearly as spacious as the second, but on a sunny day like today, most of the bar's patrons up here were on the rooftop where the bluegrass music wafted out to them. With the floor so uncrowded, I was able to return to the table with our drinks in record time.

"You think the girls could do without you for a half hour or so?"

"I think so," she said, lifting up her glass. "Cheers to my successful Nashville mission. Not once, but twice."

We clinked glasses and drank.

"Hmm. So . . . you're dancing tonight, right?"

"I am. Have to leave soon, actually. I'd be happy to get you guys in."

Her sigh was as exaggerated as all of Min's moods. If she was happy, you knew it. Excited, you knew that too. Sad? While she didn't seem sad, exactly, there was no denying she was disappointed at the moment, on behalf of not seeing me, it seemed. And, well, I shouldn't be happy about that . . .

But I was.

"I'd love to." She looked me up and down. "Trust me, I really would." I adored that twinkle in her eye. "But I think two nights of stripping might be enough for the girls. There were a few places on their hit list . . ." She trailed off.

"I get it. This is Brooke's weekend."

"And I'm just along for the ride," she said.

I smiled. "Figuratively speaking, of course."

Min laughed unrestrainedly, and I couldn't help but laugh with her. "You have a dirty mind. Occupational hazard?"

"If my occupation is being a man? Then yes."

She might have accused me of having a dirty mind, but Min looked at me as if she remembered our kiss quite clearly.

"I wish I could have spent more time with you this weekend, Min," I said, with no time to waste being coy.

"Me too." She looked so forlorn that I couldn't help it. Jumping from my stool, I stood next to her. Pulling her neck toward me, I kissed her again, wanting it to keep going forever but knowing we were in a public place.

"Mind if I stay right here?" I said, pulling the beer toward me.

"Mind?" She looked at me intensely, with a sincere expression. "If I had my way, you wouldn't leave my side until I got on the plane to go home."

"If I had my way, you wouldn't go home."

With nothing to say to that, Min took a sip of her drink. As hot as the kiss was, the fact that we had maybe fifteen minutes before never seeing each other again, maybe ever, made the afternoon bittersweet.

"This sucks." Her perfect lips formed a frown. One I was determined to turn into a smile.

"Don't cry because it's over," I said. "Smile because it happened."

She did, but it was the most pathetically sad smile I'd ever seen. I didn't try to talk her out of it. I knew exactly how she felt. As if I'd just won a million dollars only to be told I had but ten minutes to live.

Damned if I'd use those ten minutes crying into my beer. I slipped my hand around Min's waist and just under her sweater, kissed her again, and pulled her so close to me it was a wonder no one had shouted "get a room" yet.

I'd never been one for such public displays of affection, but there was a first time for everything.

CHAPTER THIRTEEN

dominica

I HATED COMING HOME FROM A VACATION, THIS ONE MORE THAN most.

As we settled into our seats on the plane, I stared out the small window. Of course it was raining. The weather matched my mood perfectly.

"Please remind me never to drink again in my entire life," Thayle said next to me.

Adjusting my travel pillow against the window, I attempted to get comfortable. "That's gonna be a bit difficult, being that you work at a vineyard."

As our wine club manager, Thayle did as much wine tasting as the rest of us.

"Ugh, then at least for a week. I'm going to hide Wednesday."

Every Wednesday since my parents started the tradition years ago, the family gathered, usually in the Wine Cellar or on its deck in good weather, to kick back. We were essentially closed to the public, since tastings stopped at five o'clock, except for VIP and club members, who, along with our own friends, always knew they could pop over on

Wednesday nights, provided they brought their own bottles. The cash register was closed and no one worked. Family rule. With weekends taken up by events, my parents realized they never got to enjoy the fruits of their labor with their friends, so the Wine Wednesday tradition was born.

"Maybe you'll feel differently in two days."

We stopped talking to listen to the captain's announcement. Brooke, sitting next to Thayle, was miraculously already asleep again. That woman could sleep anywhere. Me? Naps weren't my thing. Way too boring.

"I doubt it," I said.

Although I couldn't fall back to sleep, I closed my eyes anyway as Thayle rummaged through her backpack. As I'd done all night since the moment Hudson walked away, I conjured mental images of his kiss in the storage room. Of afterward when we talked about our childhoods, Hudson sitting so close to me I could smell him the whole time. How could a scent be so potent? A man, so freaking hot?

When I'd first walked into the bar and saw him dressed like a cowboy from head to toe, for me, I'd literally stopped walking to stare. Then he sang, his voice so perfectly smooth and sexy, focused on me the entire time.

There were a million beautiful girls down here, and though I didn't believe that he didn't enjoy his share of groupies, his attention was flattering nonetheless. At one point in the evening, he even asked if he could text me again, and of course I said yes (duh), though perhaps I wouldn't be all that surprised if he never actually texted me.

At the end of the night, as I was heading down to meet the girls, he'd given me a final quick kiss in the stairwell, and then said a goodbye to the group as he was departing for job number two, and that was the last I'd heard from him.

"You feeling okay?" Thayle asked.

My eyes popped open. "A bit of a headache, but otherwise fine."

There was another announcement, this one about the runway not yet being cleared. The same thing had happened on the way here, but we were much more annoyed by the delay then.

"I don't mean a hangover." My best friend and I looked at each other, understanding passing between us.

"I'm fine," I said. "What happens in Nashville and all that."

"I know, but . . . you really seemed to like the guy."

"What's not to like? Except maybe that he has legions of women hanging on him pretty much twenty-four seven."

"I'll admit, Hudson was pretty sexy."

"Pretty sexy?" I sat up in my seat. "Are you out of your mind? Did you actually see him?"

"You have to remember, you're the one with a thing for guys in a cowboy hat. And that to me, no man alive is sexier than Neo."

"Ugh, I hope someday I get used to you saying that about my brother."

"It's not like I'm sharing sex stories."

"Ooooh," Brooke, who I'd thought was asleep, piped in without even opening her eyes. "That would be a fun way to tease Min. Let's swap some good sex stories, Thayle."

"Oh my god, you two are gross."

They laughed. Eww.

"I'm actually surprised." Thayle unbuckled her seat belt to shove her backpack under the seat in front of her. "He seemed so into you. I thought you might actually hear from him again."

I've never met anyone quite like you.

Hudson had said this just minutes before he had to leave, as his hand cupped my cheek, his thumb caressing my face, sounding as if he'd meant it at the time. He'd capped the statement with a too-brief kiss, and I'd stupidly believed him.

"At least we have the wedding," I said.

Thayle looked at me like I was nuts. "What does that have to do with Hudson?"

"You know, something to distract me, to look forward to."

"I swear your mind never stops. What would you do with an actual, I don't know, week of downtime? With nothing exciting planned?"

A fate worse than death. "I don't know and don't plan to try it anytime soon."

Thayle looked as if she wanted to say something, but instead she unbuckled her seat belt again. "Forgot my granola bar," she said, reaching for her backpack again. I felt bad for the person in front of her. This was only the beginning. She'd be in and out of that thing fifty times before we landed.

Sitting back in my seat, I closed my eyes and again pictured Hudson dressed as a cop. Then I reimagined the second time he tied my hands behind my back. And Hudson asking if I wanted him and Oliver to come with us. Our kiss at Skull's. The way he'd grabbed my hair, pulling me toward him. And since I was dwelling on that, the storage room. He'd lifted me up as if I weighed practically nothing, which was definitely not true. I liked Devine Bakery's donuts too much for that.

My phone buzzed. I'd thought I'd put it on airplane mode already.

Morning sunshine ☀ *Hope I didn't miss u?*

Holy shit. I elbowed Thayle. "Look!"

I shoved my phone at her. We stared at each other for a second before she handed it back. "Well, text him. Hurry before we take off."

"So quickly?"

"This from the woman who said she loved Hudson's directness. That he didn't play games or screw around."

"Okay." I fired off a quick text.

On the runway now, delayed

He immediately wrote back.

Late night, didn't want to disturb you. Figured you got in early.

I held my phone out to show Thayle that text too. Heart beating a bit faster now, I sat up in my seat. "He didn't want to disturb me."

We had returned to our rental house early because of the early morning flight. But that hadn't stopped me from waking up twice to check my phone.

"Now what do I say?"

Thayle leaned over as the captain made another announcement. We were finally cleared for takeoff. He instructed the flight attendants to make final preparations.

"Whatever you do, be quick about it," Thayle said.

Shit. My brain wasn't working that fast so early in the morning after the kind of long weekend we'd just had.

What the hell. Couldn't go wrong with the truth: *About to take off. Glad you texted.*

Did you doubt I would?

That was an easy one. *Honestly, yes*

I couldn't help but smile at his frowny face. It was hard to believe that a guy like Hudson was actually into me this much. I could understand hanging out while I was down here, but to continue to talk after it was over? Honestly, I hadn't expected it.

No sad faces allowed. Text you when I land?

You better. Safe travels, sunshine.

"I officially have a pet name." I showed Thayle the phone again.

"Oh wow, you really have gone off the deep end." She smiled. "I honestly can't remember seeing you like this with a guy before."

I fired off one last text before responding to her.

Thanks 🤠

When I looked up, Thayle was staring at me.

"What?" I asked as we began to pull out of the gate.

"I don't know. It's just . . . you're lit up like a group of girls on their last tasting of the day."

I nodded to Brooke. "After vodka roadies?"

Brooke groaned. I totally knew she was awake.

"I still can't believe we did that," she said opening her eyes. "How we thought water bottles filled with vodka between wineries was a good idea, I'll never know. So your cowboy texted?"

"He did." My cheeks hurt from smiling.

"Now what? Last I looked, he lived in Nashville," Brooke said.

"I hadn't really thought very hard about that. I've been too busy closing my eyes and remembering him half naked."

"Half? I'd say mostly naked," Thayle said.

"Well, I've seen your fiancés naked, so it's only fair.

Although I'm not sure running around the house as a toddler is quite the same thing."

That got a chuckle from both of my future sisters-in-law.

"He is hot," Thayle said.

"You think?" I asked sarcastically. "And he can dance, something I've always wished for in a guy. And he sings. And is a really, really good kisser."

"And lives in Nashville," Brooke, the party pooper, reminded me.

"That's probably a good thing. Can you imagine your brothers' reactions to his profession?" Thayle asked.

The thought had crossed my mind.

"Jesus, no," Brooke said. "They'd lose it. Speaking of, are we keeping the details on the DL?"

"Nah. I don't want you guys to ever have to lie for me. We have nothing to be ashamed of."

"I just thought," Brooke said, "maybe go light on some of the finer points."

"Like the fact that he handcuffed Min and tied her hands behind her back all within a twenty-four-hour span?"

"Exactly." Brooke readjusted her pillow to go back to sleep.

"I mean, the fewer details we can give, the better," I agreed. "Who do you think would lose their minds the most?"

"Cos, for sure," Brooke said.

As the eldest, he probably was the most protective of me. But I disagreed. "I think Marco."

Thayle agreed with me. "For sure. He's done too much himself to trust any guy, particularly one who shoves his schlong in women's faces for a living."

"Thayle." I slapped her on the arm. "Please."

She was unrepentant. "It's true."

"Speaking of schlongs," Brooke said, closing her eyes again. "I'm exhausted."

Thayle and I exchanged a look.

"What does being exhausted have to do with schlongs?" I wondered.

"Only a virgin would ask that," Brooke answered.

"Speaking of, Nashville would have been a perfect time to change that status," Thayle said.

"It would. And Hudson might actually be worthy of the honor. But at this point, I'm really thinking it should be more than a one-night stand."

"Who knows, maybe it will be. Maybe he'll come visit his aunt Dorothy."

"I doubt it. The guy works three jobs. Most likely, I'll never see him again."

"Which is why you're so excited he texted you?"

I braced myself as the plane roared down the runway. Takeoffs sucked. Instead of answering, I made a face at Thayle, who also hated takeoffs. We were silent, but I couldn't help thinking about our conversation. What was the point of being excited? Hudson was a vacation romance, nothing more.

Still, I looked back at my phone, smiling at "safe travels, sunshine."

As Brooke always said, *carpe fucking diem*. One day at a time. We weren't guaranteed another one, might as well enjoy this one while it lasted.

CHAPTER FOURTEEN
hudson

"Excuse me?"

I turned to find a pretty brunette at the front of the stage. She was on the shorter side, light brown hair and startling green eyes. What a combination. Unusual, for sure.

"Give me a sec," I said, adjusting the mic.

"All yours," I said to Jeff, the lead singer of the band about to play. If I wasn't off to Whiskey Soul for Encore, I'd stay to listen a bit. These guys were fantastic, probably one of the best playing on Broadway at the moment. "Have a great set."

"Thanks, Hudson," he said as I tossed my guitar on my back and climbed down from the stage.

"Sorry about that," I said to the brunette, moving to a quiet corner. "How's it going?"

"Good." She smiled, glancing toward the bar. I did the same, which was when I noticed her waiting girlfriends. The reason for her visit suddenly became clear.

Crap. This was one of the worst parts of the job.

"You were amazing up there," she said.

"Thanks." Knowing where this was headed, I tried to cut it short, but she added, "You mentioned being a whiskey guy onstage. I'd love to buy you one. As a thank-you for the music."

"Unfortunately, I have another gig to get to," I said. "But thanks for the offer. And the compliment." I'd begun to walk away when she stopped me.

"Another time?"

"Sorry. Girlfriend," I lied. Hated to do it, but I'd found that using any other reason kept the door open.

Her hand dropped. "I am so sorry," she said. "Thanks again for the entertainment."

"No problem. Have a great night. I'd stay for these guys," I said, seeing her friends getting up. "You won't find a better band."

Smiling, she hurried away.

"Thanks for that," Jeff said. I turned back toward the stage, where he and the guys were setting up.

"She's a looker," he said of the woman who'd just hit on me.

"She is," I agreed, an image of Min popping into my head as it had done nearly a hundred times all week. This woman paled in comparison.

"Who's the lucky girlfriend?"

"Not sure if I'd call her that." We'd texted a few times this week, but "girlfriend" was more than a stretch. "Woman I met last weekend. Came down for a bachelorette party."

"Ahhh, so she's seen you in a thong already?"

I laughed. "She has."

"And she didn't run away screaming?"

"Not quite. But she did get on a plane back to New York."

"You like her?"

Understatement of the century. "I do. But she's in New York. I'm here. So . . ." I shrugged.

"We spent a few years in the city before coming to play down here. Not dying to do that again anytime soon."

"Actually, she's from upstate. Not far from my parents."

"No shit? Quite a coincidence."

"Sort of. My aunt who lives in her hometown told her about the show. She gave her my phone number."

"Sounds like it's time for a visit home, maybe?"

Funnily enough, I'd been thinking the exact same thing. It was too soon, though. We'd only met a week ago. "Maybe. Hey, I don't want to keep you. Sorry I can't stay. Duty calls."

"If by *duty* you mean crawling all over beautiful women screaming for you, then sure."

"Any time you want to give it a shot, we're hiring," I said.

Jeff patted his stomach. "Too many cheeseburgers in here for that. I'll leave the six-pack abs to you. But thanks for the offer."

"Any time." I saluted him and walked away, looking back at the woman who'd apparently decided to stay. She was pretty. Really pretty, in fact. A week ago, I might have even taken her up on her offer. But today, there was only one brunette I wanted to have a whiskey with.

Heading out of the bar, I walked down the street. It was only three blocks to Whiskey Soul, though I was a bit early.

It wasn't called Whiskey Soul for no reason. Originally a whiskey bar, they still had some of the best on the strip. I would take that drink after all, but solo. By the time I'd walked inside, I'd made a decision. I didn't know the bartender, but the owner had talked about hiring to lighten the load.

"Hi there," I said. The bartender was barely twenty-one. Time to test the kid out. "Can I get an Auchentoshan Three Wood, neat, with a water back?"

He didn't flinch. "Sure thing."

Pulling out my phone, I looked at our last messages. So far Min and I had talked about our week's schedules, neither of us holding back about how much we enjoyed last weekend, but that was about it.

I texted her.

Hey sunshine

I loved that Min responded immediately when she had her phone. I'd told her as much, and she'd said she hated when people took forever to respond. That it drove her nuts. So I'd told her, when I wasn't working, I'd do the same.

Hey yourself, not working?

In between gigs, you?

Just closed the wine barn

Perfect. I sent a text back: *Quick video chat?*

I hadn't seen her since last Saturday night, when I walked away from her table.

Sure!

Sitting at the end of the bar, I was thankful to be in between bands, though I didn't know how long the quiet would last. I could go outside if needed.

"On the house," the bartender said, pushing my glass toward me. So he knew I worked upstairs. I'd have to tell the owner he had a winner on his hands. "Thanks."

Clicking the call button, I waited for her to answer, feeling like I was walking onstage for the first time.

"Well, hello there, stranger," she said.

Fuck.

She couldn't possibly look more adorable. Min wore a thick cream sweater, appropriate for the temps up there, with her hair piled on top of her head in a messy bun.

"You look like a hotter than hell snow bunny who just got off the slopes."

She laughed. "And you look like some sexy Nashville country singer about to get scooped up by his adoring fans."

"Only one adoring fan I'm looking to get scooped up by."

"Oh really? Who might that be?"

"I'm looking at her. Finally. It's been too long."

"Exactly one week," she said.

I could see wine bottles behind her. "Show me the Barn."

Min loved that place. I knew from how excited she got whenever she talked about it.

"Okay, hold on." She turned the phone. "So . . . this is the main tasting room. We just redecorated a few years ago."

As she showed me around, I marveled at the place. No wonder she loved working there. It looked like a cross between what you'd expect from a wine barn and a Tuscan villa.

"And these are our featured wines. Each of them is named after a woman in the Grado family."

"Where's yours?" I asked.

"There it is," she said. "Min Bubbly. It pops out of the glass"—she put on her sales voice—"with notes of lemons, limes, and peaches. A delicate balance of flavor and body, this is a wine that will have you coming back for more."

She turned the phone back to herself.

"That seems to be named perfectly. I agree on the coming back for more part." Her eyes told me that the call had definitely taken a turn. I'd have said more, except for the fact that I was in a public bar. "I wish you were still down here," I said, taking a sip of whiskey.

She sat down at the tasting bar. "I wish you were up here. Maybe time for a visit?"

Though she'd said it jokingly, I could tell Min wasn't joking at all.

And neither was I. "It'll be a bitch to clear my schedule."

"I bet." That she seemed disappointed gave me the courage to say fuck it and just do it. I'd thought of nothing else since the second I walked away from her. Something about Min pulled me to her, and it wasn't just the fact that she fit so perfectly against me. I craved more of her kisses and wanted to go back to the night we met. If I'd only known she wasn't the bride . . .

"But I could do it," I said. I could see from the corner of my eye the band was going to start up soon. I was running out of time.

Min stared back at me, her surprise evident. I tightened my grip on the phone, my heart racing.

"If you want," I blurted. Min stared back at me through the phone, her surprise evident.

For a terrible second, I thought she might say no.

"This is a total long shot but," she hesitated. "My brother's wedding is in a few weeks. Over Valentine's Day weekend . . ."

Whew. Though I was booked solid, always. And that was just a few weeks away. But as crazy as the idea was, I didn't even consider saying no. No risk, no reward.

"You're trying to tell me . . . you don't already have a date?" I teased.

"Oh, that's right," she said. "I do. Almost forgot. Never mind."

"Smart-ass," I said, grinning widely. "Count me in as your plus-one."

I loved that Min beamed at that. "Are you serious?"

"Of course. I'm due for a trip home. My mom will be thrilled." I shrugged. "It'll take a bit of juggling with my schedule, but more than worth it."

"To see your mom?" She was still smiling broadly.

"Yes, to see my mom," I said just as the band began. "Do you have a few more minutes? I'll move out of here," I shouted.

"Definitely."

After tossing a bill on the bar, I grabbed both my guitar and whiskey and made my way upstairs. It was early enough none of the guys would be here yet. Heading into the dressing room, I flipped on the light and settled into a seat.

"Back," I said, setting the whiskey down.

"Where are you?" Min asked.

"Dressing room at Whiskey Soul. I was in the bar downstairs between gigs. Wasn't worth going back home."

"You work nonstop," she said.

"Pot, meet kettle." I knew from our discussions she basically lived in the Wine Barn.

"Guilty as charged." As she spoke, Min's tone changed. Something was up.

I looked behind me. The costumes.

"Min," I started, knowing this conversation would have to happen. Significant others often struggled with this lifestyle, and I didn't blame them.

"I have to tell you something," she blurted.

I hated how scared she suddenly looked. Was this not about the stripping?

"What's up?"

"I—" She clamped her mouth shut, sighed, and then started again. "You shouldn't come all the way up here . . ."

My chest, suddenly heavy, tightened. I knew this was too good to be true.

". . . without knowing something."

"Whatever it is, I can assure you it doesn't matter." I grabbed the whiskey.

"This might. So . . ."

Jesus, had she murdered someone? I couldn't imagine what she was so worried about telling me.

"I'm a virgin."

Nope. Decidedly not murder. "And that matters because . . . ?"

She shrugged. "Because you're flying all the way up here to see me. I just thought it was important for you to know. I'm not saving myself for marriage, exactly. It's just, my brothers kind of scared me into not giving it up too easily. And then no one seemed . . ."

I grinned. "Worthy?"

Thankfully, Min laughed. "I suppose."

"I really don't give a shit about that. It changes nothing. Despite the fact that I want you so badly it's literally all I can think about."

Again, her expression changed. This time to absolute panic. So I clarified.

"Honestly, Min, I don't care if you—"

"So," she interrupted, "I can't believe you're actually coming to the wedding."

Something was up. That something appeared on the screen behind her. And he didn't look happy.

"Sorry about the nosy nelly behind me. He has no boundaries. Marco, meet Hudson. Hudson, Marco."

The second-oldest brother. Vice president of Grado Valley Vineyards and, according to Min, the loose cannon of the family. Who had likely overheard what I'd said about wanting Min. Great.

I smiled. "Nice to meet you."

He did not smile back. "Same."

His tone, and expression, said the very opposite. Min had said her brothers were overprotective, and judging from what she just told me, it seemed they had a heavy influence on her as well. Winning them over wasn't going to be easy.

"I've got to get ready for the show," I said, knowing it would be a hell of a lot easier to win them over in person. "And a schedule to clear."

Marco moved out of the screen, but from Min's expression, it was clear he hadn't gone far.

"I seriously can't believe you're coming. I'll text you the details."

"Deal. I'll talk to my boss here tonight and then take a look at my singing gigs that weekend. I'm sure you'll be busy in the days before the wedding . . ."

"Come for as long as you can."

The look we exchanged was more meaningful than any words we could say. She wanted me up there, and I did too. Not that this could work long term with us in two different places, but I wouldn't think about that now. I'd take it day by day.

"Will do. Talk soon."

"Ok. Have a . . ." She hesitated. "Never mind. I don't think I want you to have a good show."

With Marco lurking, now wasn't the time. But I'd reassure her later.

"It's just a job," was all I said now. "Talk tomorrow?" Now that I had her on video, text messages just wouldn't cut it.

"For sure."

"Good night, sunshine." With a wink, I hung up the phone.

I had a trip to plan.

CHAPTER FIFTEEN

dominica

"Are you fucking kidding me?" Marco was furious.

Of all the rotten times for my brother to sulk into the tasting room. It was my fault for completely forgetting he'd been back there. Marco's office was in the Wine Cellar, but periodically he came here when it got "too busy" over there. Which made zero sense. It wasn't like his office was plopped in the middle of the tasting room.

On the other hand, I sort of understood. There was a quiet peacefulness to this space that couldn't be found anywhere else on the estate. Except the actual vineyards. Or maybe out by the lake. Actually, there were a lot of quiet spots, but this one was my favorite. And Marco's too sometimes, unfortunately.

"What?" I snapped, knowing exactly what his problem was.

"'I want you so badly it's literally all I can think about'?"

Yeah, bad timing.

"Oh, that's rich. You of all people are going to lecture me? The same guy who has a new girlfriend every week. Really?"

"First of all," my smug asshole of a brother said, "I don't have a new girlfriend every week. Second of all, you're better than me."

Talk about taking the wind out of my sails. But I wasn't ready to give up the fight yet, mainly because of his tone. "Okay, so maybe girlfriend was the wrong word."

His glare might have scared other people, but not me.

"'I've got to get ready for the show,'" he mocked. "It was pretty clear by the costumes behind him exactly what kind of show he meant. Real classy."

It wasn't as if this was news to Marco. He and my brothers had poked and prodded me, Thayle, and Brooke to no end, and managed to put together a fairly clear picture of what was going on with me and Hudson—and what he did for a living. To say they weren't thrilled that I'd been texting with a guy who happened to also be a male entertainer would be a colossal understatement. But I'd nipped their judgments about Hudson in the bud by saying I refused to talk about it.

Until now.

"You know what's classy," I shot back. "Bringing a woman home, sleeping with her, and then leaving her in your bed to text another woman."

Marco's eyes narrowed. "I really have to get out of here."

Thayle might kill me for mentioning that one, but he deserved it. Truth was, with Neo and Marco living together in a lakefront cottage on the property, I'd heard a lot of Marco stories from Thayle (sometimes via bigmouth Neo), far more than I would usually admit to Marco. That particular incident was just a few weeks ago. Thayle happened to be in the kitchen when Marco pulled that particular stunt.

"Like I said, Min, you're better than me."

"And by 'better,' you mean I haven't had sex. At the age of twenty-five. Thanks."

"Don't you dare lay that on me. I never told you not to have sex." He thought about that for a second. "I mean, it's not a bad idea. Might as well go the distance at this point."

"Nice, Marco."

With it being a Friday afternoon after closing time, he went for an already opened bottle, poured two glasses of wine, and handed one to me. "I'm really not trying to start a fight."

I took the wine. "Are you fucking kidding me?" I said, tossing his words back to him. "That's not exactly a great opener unless fighting is the goal."

"The goal is having you rethink talking to this guy."

I leaned against the bar, wishing I had some backup. Marco was relentless and would not let go of this easily.

"I'm not a kid anymore, Marco. In case you haven't noticed. I run this place"—I waved my arms—"almost single-handedly. Give me a little bit of credit."

"I give you all the credit in the world," my brother said. "You know I adore you. Which is why I don't think a guy who takes off his clothes for a living is the best fit for you."

I tried a different angle. "He's also an incredibly talented singer."

"Who has to strip for women, and bartend, to make ends meet."

"Since when are you such a snob?"

"I'm not being a snob, just giving you the facts."

"I guess we don't care that he's incredibly nice, and kind, and thoughtful. None of that matters?"

Marco took a sip of his wine, preparing his attack. "How about the fact that he lives in Nashville doing all of these 'incredibly nice' things like stripping? And you're here."

How could I love and hate someone so much all at once? Of all my brothers, he drove me the craziest. I hadn't planned on telling him until it was one hundred percent definite, but might as well rip the Band-Aid off now.

"Not for long," I shot back. "He's coming up. To the wedding."

"Like hell he is," Marco spouted, his temper getting the best of him. "There is no fucking way you're bringing a stranger, a fucking male stripper, to Cosimo's wedding."

Over the years, I'd learned that yelling back at Marco would get us exactly nowhere. "Maybe lower your voice. I can hear you perfectly well. And please stop calling him that."

"It's true," he shot back.

"I don't call you 'the VP.' It's a job. Not his identity. And I am taking him to the wedding. I honestly think you'll like him."

Marco snorted. "And then what, are you going to date the guy from New York? Fly down to see some of his shows, maybe?"

That was enough. When he got like this, there was no talking to him. Marco would rather swim headfirst into a hungry shark's mouth than back down or admit he was wrong.

"I'm done," I said. "If you want to have a conversation about this, fine. But this is not a conversation."

With that, I took the half-empty bottle of wine and my glass and marched into my office, slamming the door. He wouldn't come after me. Marco liked to instigate fights, but he knew when he'd pushed me too far.

Now it was just a matter of waiting for the shitstorm. Because he would run right to Neo, or Cos. Whoever he could find first. Within an hour, every damn Grado on the estate would know Hudson was coming to the wedding. Which meant I should probably talk to Brooke first. She wouldn't be as close-minded as my brother, but still it seemed prudent to give her a heads up.

I pulled my phone toward me, poured more wine into my glass, and called my future sister-in-law, hoping to find an ally in this looming battle.

CHAPTER SIXTEEN

"YOUR FAVORITE COLOR?"

"Green," I said, shifting my position.

I'd been holding the phone up to see Min for over an hour. It was rare for us to find this much time to talk. Between our schedules, the best we could usually do was text, and almost never at the same time. During the day, she was working. At night, I was working. Thanks to an early afternoon gig, no Encore show on Wednesdays and a canceled bartending shift, we now had a full two hours. Unfortunately, with it being Wednesday night, Min would have to head back to the estate, where Brooke and Cosimo's wedding planning was in full swing. But in the meantime, I'd take what I could get.

"Let me guess, yours is blue?"

"How did you know?" she asked, settled in on her bed.

Min still lived with her parents. Although I couldn't imagine such a thing, having never returned home from college, Min said she loved being pampered and fed. And though she'd considered moving into one of the on-property cottages like her brothers, to make it a quick walk to work, Min had said there was no other good reason to move out.

"Lucky guess," I said.

"Okay, something a bit deeper. What are you most afraid of?"

"From favorite color to biggest fear. That is quite a leap."

As always, Min's expressions hid nothing. She was relaxed, happy. I couldn't help being pleased, not that all the credit was mine. But yesterday she had told me she was "beyond excited" for my trip up there. I couldn't have said it better myself. The thought of being able to kiss her again had been keeping me up at night. In a good way.

"I thought of it because of what you said earlier, about being worried to meet my brothers. It's hard to imagine someone like you being afraid of anything."

"Someone like me? You mean incredibly handsome with a great voice and even better dance moves?" I teased her.

"You forgot humble."

"That too."

"No, I mean, just . . . that you're so confident about everything you do."

I thought about her question. I used to fear failing, coming down here and not making it. But I didn't anymore. "I fear losing my love of music," I said instead.

"What do you mean?"

"As long as I can remember, songs were a way for me to learn about myself. To make sense of the world. Being able to share them, even between covers and not more than once or twice a gig, was a dream to me. The bigger dream was being able to share only my songs to a wider audience.

To make a career out of it." I shook my head. "But now I just don't know."

"What don't you know?"

"If I want that."

"Because it seems too daunting?"

"Nah, that's not it. If I really wanted to hit it big, I'd just keep at it. Keep playing, keep making connections, and eventually I'd get there. At least to a level I could make a full-time living out of it, if not a record deal. The only true way to fail is to quit."

"Then what don't you know about?"

This was harder to put into words. "I don't know that I want to write songs and sing for money anymore. I've been thinking to accept fewer singing gigs. One or two a week maybe. But," I sighed, "I'm just not sure."

"Well . . ." Min thought about it. I could almost see the steam coming from her ears. "If cutting back would make you love writing and singing more, taking some of the pressure of having to do it off you, sounds to me like a win-win. Why the hesitation? Does it feel like giving up?"

"Maybe a little. My parents were pretty pissed about me coming here, 'throwing away an education' and all that. But to me, if you hate waking up on Monday mornings, what's the point?"

"From someone who loves their job, I couldn't agree more. When I hear people talk about being so happy it's the weekend or dreading the end of it, I feel badly for them. But I know it's not always practical to just up and quit. To find your passion and actually make a living doing it."

"Exactly," I agreed.

"But with you," she continued, "you know your passion but don't necessarily want to do it on the clock. I could see with a creative endeavor like that, having to do it to pay the bills might take some of the enjoyment from it."

I couldn't agree more.

"Speaking of passion," I said, knowing she would head out soon. "I noticed when you sent me the inn reservations, both of our names were on the room."

She smiled. "I took the liberty of changing my reservation to a king and adding you to mine. Of course, if you want your own—"

"Are you kidding me? You're not going to be able to keep me off you, Dominica. There are a lot of ways we can have fun without sex." She opened her mouth, and I shut her down immediately, knowing what she was going to say. "Don't you dare apologize."

That Min didn't say anything then told me I'd been right. We looked at one another, a silent understanding passing between us.

"I'll keep the one room," she said.

"You better."

"Just out of curiosity, what exactly are you planning?"

Since she asked . . . "I plan to remove your bridesmaid's dress and familiarize myself with every inch of you." I paused. "With my tongue."

Min's mouth fell open. I wanted to kiss her so fucking bad.

"That sounds"—she swallowed—"acceptable."

"Good." I was hard as a rock now. Not unlike every time I thought of Min and our storage room kiss. Time to cool things down. Min had to leave soon.

With a deep breath and a shift in position, I turned the tables on her. "You never told me your biggest fear."

"Oh god, we don't have the time now," she laughed. "There are too many."

"We can talk about it in person," I said. "One week."

"I still can't believe you're coming. You sure you don't want to come Friday night?"

Though Min had invited me to the rehearsal dinner, I figured it was best that she spend that time with her family. Besides, if I didn't give my mother at least a few days of face time before heading to Lake Geneva, where the wedding was taking place, she wouldn't be happy.

"I'm sure. Mom is excited to have me home. I'll be there in time for the wedding."

"What if there's a snowstorm?"

"I've driven in snow most of my life. You honestly think that would keep me from you?"

She seemed relieved by that. "I have the room for Saturday and Sunday nights. And a cottage back on our property after that until Wednesday, when you're leaving. Does that work?"

The last thing I wanted to think about was leaving her before I even got there. "Yep."

"I still can't believe you took a whole week off."

"I wish I could have taken more," I said. As it was, trying to clear my schedule for three jobs had me promising more shifts to more people than I cared to think about.

"Are we nuts?" she blurted suddenly. "I mean, we met exactly twice. We hardly know each other. And now you're—"

"Flying home to see you and essentially be introduced to your entire family, including three overprotective brothers, at once? I don't know about you, but I definitely am. Also, it's three times."

"That first time doesn't count."

"The time when I handcuffed you to a chair? Doesn't count?"

"No, because you thought I was getting married."

"Doesn't mean we didn't meet. Or that I wasn't drawn to you from the second I came out of the back room."

"Get out of here. You were not."

"I was, Min."

"You perform for room after room of women ready to throw their panties at you. And you picked *me* out of the crowd?"

"That's exactly the reason I'm flying from Nashville to New York. I know what I want. And I want you."

"I just don't get it."

"I'm going to change that," I said, and she looked at me, not understanding. "Any doubts you have about why you are so amazing. If anyone here is lucky, it's me."

She made a not-so-ladylike sound.

"You don't strike me as the kind of woman who doubts herself often."

"I'm not. Just with you. I mean, look at you."

I flipped the video around on the phone, did what she said, and then turned it back around. "Okay, now what?"

"You are such an ass. I wish I didn't have to, but I've gotta run. The family will kill me if I'm late for *Star Wars* trivia night. If it wasn't for me, they'd never win."

"*Star Wars* girl, huh?"

She smiled. "I am." And then, "Oh no. Please don't tell me you're a Trekkie."

"Guilty as charged."

She made a face. "Oh well. I guess we can try to overcome that.

And speaking of overcoming, don't worry about my brothers. I will have a nice chat with them before next weekend."

I kept my mouth shut for now, knowing that a chat

probably wouldn't do much good, since, if it were me, I wouldn't want my sister dating a guy who spent his time grinding on other women either. The last thing I wanted Min to do was worry on her brother's wedding day about how they'd take to me. I must have asked her fifty times before I booked my flight if she was sure. I could come home another time. But she'd insisted she was glad to have a date, couldn't wait to see me, and that her brothers wouldn't be a problem.

"Have a good night, sunshine."

The nickname suited her well.

"Same to you," she said.

After we hung up, I waited exactly three seconds before deciding now was the perfect time for a shower. Putting aside thoughts of the Grado brothers, I'd concentrate on Min instead. On how adorable she looked and how much I couldn't wait to see her in person. And to get her alone.

It was going to be some trip home, that was for sure.

CHAPTER SEVENTEEN

dominica

"Min, can we talk to you a second?"

As soon as I saw both Marco and Neo behind the bar with him, my instinct was to tell Cos no. They were about to gang up on me, and I couldn't help but wonder at their timing. Aside from a few games of trivia, tonight had mostly been last-minute wedding prep. My parents were here chatting with a few of their old favorite VIP customers by the fireplace. They were looking relaxed and happy in retirement, finally, and I was glad for them.

But not glad for me. I was totally cornered.

"Come on, just a sec," Marco said. Reluctantly I got up, telling Maci, our admin and logistics lead, I'd be right back.

"We don't want a fight," Neo started as I walked behind the main tasting bar. "But we're concerned."

Anyone else might have been intimidated by three burly men who looked like they were right out of a mob movie. Especially since all three glared at me as if a fight was exactly what they were prepared for. But I was used to their tactics, even if they ganged up on me, like they were doing now.

"Which I appreciate," I said sarcastically. "And honestly, I wanted to talk to you guys anyway, so now's as good a time as any." I launched right in. "Please don't be assholes to Hudson next weekend. Seriously."

They exchanged a "crap, we'd planned on doing just that" look.

"We're never assholes," Neo started, but I stopped him immediately.

"The summer between sophomore and junior year you and Marco purposely took my boyfriend waterskiing knowing he couldn't swim. And he was too afraid to tell you no. So don't tell me you're never assholes to my boyfriends."

"First of all, he was wearing a life jacket," Marco said, swirling his wine.

"Second of all," Neo chimed in, standing next to him. "We spotted him and watched him like a hawk. The guy was never in danger of drowning."

"But you did succeed in scaring him shitless."

The two of them exchanged a look, Neo doing a much better job of hiding his amusement. The pair were clearly unrepentant.

"You're not any better," I said to Cos, who was clearly happy to be left out of the conversation.

"If you're talking about the bachelor party incident, maybe your ex shouldn't have been ogling the pretty bartender," Cos said.

"You're telling me since meeting Brooke you haven't once noticed another woman existed? Come on, Cos. He literally just glanced at her. She was wearing a hot pink crop top, for god's sakes. How do you not look?"

"Easy. You remember two of your girlfriend's three

brothers are watching you. It just would have taken a little bit of self-control."

"You're missing the point. If the three of you are going to stand here and tell me, with a straight face, you haven't been assholes to my boyfriends more often than not, I can't take you seriously."

Marco and Neo were quick to disagree, but Cos, ever the peacemaker, relented. "We could be a bit much," he said amidst Marco and Neo's protests. "But you have to admit, we have a good reason this time. The guy spends his weekends taking his clothes off for other women. And you think we're going to be okay with that?"

I needed more wine for this. I looked behind the bar for an open bottle, but Marco, sensing what I was doing, found one for me and filled my glass. He could be the biggest jerk of all three of them, but he also managed to be incredibly astute and thoughtful too.

"Thanks," I muttered and took a calming sip. It took everything I had to keep from losing my temper. I took a deep breath, then evenly pointed out, "What matters is what I'm okay with. Not you."

"And you're okay with that, for real?" Neo asked.

Truthfully, no. Every night I knew he was working with Encore, my stomach was in knots thinking about it. "I guess I should be worried about him looking sexy onstage as he sings to scores of adoring female fans too?"

"That would make me jealous," Marco admitted. Of course it would. He was the jealous type. But I couldn't chastise him for it. I never thought I was, until Hudson. So I pointed out the obvious.

"We aren't even dating exclusively, so this is all nonsense."

"Exactly. You met him one weekend. You hardly know

the guy and will probably be broken up soon anyway. So why take him to the wedding?" Marco asked.

"I'm taking him as a date. So I don't have to go alone," I tossed back. "And watch all of the happy couples, including you with my best friend," I said to Neo, "who I'd otherwise be hanging out with."

There, I said it. Was I jealous of Neo and Thayle's relationship? I liked to think I wasn't. But there was no point denying our dynamic had changed since they started dating.

"I love you both," I added, to make sure he understood. "And I love you together. It makes me happy as a clam. But I can't pretend it doesn't sometimes get a little lonely too."

"Marco's going alone," Cos said, as if that had anything to do with Neo and Thayle.

"Actually," Marco hedged.

That was when I really got pissed. "Are you serious? You're taking one of your floozy dates to the wedding and have the balls to talk to me about Hudson?"

Not one person here could argue that Marco didn't have a terrible track record with women. We hardly ever saw one of his "girlfriends" more than once. If ever there was a love 'em and loose 'em guy, it was my brother.

"I didn't know you were bringing someone," Cos said. "Maybe you should let Neo and me talk. It does seem a bit hypocritical."

"A bit?" I rolled my eyes. "The point is, there are different standards for you than for me. Case in point."

"Of course there are. You're a woman," Marco said. At which point Neo whistled and Cos backed up. My jaw, still on the floor, refused to close. "I'm sorry, just stating the obvious."

"What the hell does my gender have to do with anything?"

"Just that . . ." He realized he'd gone too far. "You know, you can get . . ." He stopped. Even Neo and Cos were no longer on his side. For now.

"Pregnant? Is that what you wanted to say? Really rich, Marco, since you know that isn't possible in my case. And even if it was, to suggest that I am not responsible enough to use birth control, or worse, that you are somehow more responsible because of your gender?" I shook my head. "I'm done with this conversation."

"Ignore him," Cos said. For a change, Marco didn't interrupt. He knew well enough to shut up now. Even Mom, who didn't think Hudson was a great idea either, would have given him a good tongue-lashing for saying something so stupid. "You can take whoever you want to the wedding, Min. We're just trying to protect you. Knowing men," he shrugged, "we want better for you."

"Better than what?" I asked.

Everyone looked at Marco, who pretended to be offended.

"How did this end up a Marco bashfest?" he asked.

"Pretty sure you know how." Knowing my brothers, even Marco, were coming from a good place, I softened my tone, if not my message. "I love that you love me enough to care. But I'm a twenty-five-year-old woman who's made pretty responsible decisions when it comes to the opposite sex, more so than you all did when you were single. So why you're doubting my judgment now, I don't know. But please stop. Please be nice and don't make this a thing. It's about Cos and Brooke next weekend. Period. End of story."

None of them looked happy. But Cos did come to me

and put his arm around my shoulders. “We love you, Min. That’s all.”

“And I love you too. Just trust me for a change, okay? Hudson isn’t the guy you think he is.”

Unfortunately, given their expressions, I didn’t think I convinced any of them to actually give Hudson a chance. But with any luck, they wouldn’t be total dicks to him either.

“We do trust you,” Neo said. “Just not him.”

As I’d thought. But I didn’t want to argue about it anymore. This was about Cos and Brooke, and I wouldn’t let anything take away from that. “No more Hudson talk. Be nice to him at the wedding, and I won’t tell Mom that you’re planning to spring the brewery idea on her and Dad after the honeymoon.”

My brothers, Marco especially, had been pitching the idea of an onsite brewery for ages. When we first took over, Cosimo, as proprietor, shut down any talk of it, knowing we needed to concentrate on the transition. Our parents had always been against the idea, but we’d finally come to the conclusion that it was time.

We had the space. We had the capital. It could really make Grado stand out with only a handful of winery-brewery operations on the lake. Marco had been doing a ton of research over the past year or so, and he felt we were ready to move forward. But it was going to be a fight even though the decisions were now ours, as owners, and not our parents’. Still, no one wanted to make them angry, to let them think we didn’t take our legacy seriously.

“You wouldn’t,” Marco said, outraged.

Well, no, I wouldn’t tell them right before the wedding. My brothers knew that. But I wanted them to know I was serious about them being nice to Hudson. Or at least giving him a chance.

"You never know." I smiled at him, Cos jabbing me in the ribs.

"Tell him you're kidding," he said.

I would, but I was still mad enough about his "woman" comment to keep my stubborn mouth shut on that matter. "I will say this. If you don't make Hudson feel welcome, the wrath of Dominica will be unleashed."

"Ooooh," Neo teased as Marco and Cosimo laughed.

The fight was over. For now.

CHAPTER EIGHTEEN

hudson

"Hey, Mom."

It was only seven a.m., and somehow the jet lag hadn't hit. I should have been sleeping, usually did on days off. Maybe it was the strange environment. Or familiar environment. Mom hadn't changed a thing in my old room yet.

"Morning, sweetie." She poured me a cup of coffee as I walked into the kitchen. It was good to be home. "Your dad left for work already," she said. Last night Mom told me she'd taken the day off to spend it with me.

"I figured." I sat at the kitchen table.

"What's wrong?"

"Nothing," I said, knowing she wouldn't believe me. If Mom got it in her head that something was wrong, I'd be better off making something up than telling her I was fine. "I'm not used to being up this early, especially with the time change."

She sat across from me. "It's something else," she said. "Last night you were on cloud nine to be home, excited to see this girl. Today, something's up."

"I'm still on cloud nine to see this girl," I said, taking a sip of what tasted like home.

"But?"

There was no but. Or maybe there was a little but. "The wedding."

After my flight got in, the three of us went to dinner. I told both of my parents all about Min, and while my dad didn't say much, as usual, my mother seemed pretty excited. She'd love nothing more than to see me settled down and didn't even pretend to hide the fact.

"It's a high-pressure first date, that's for sure," Mom said.

I hadn't realized it even bothered me until Mom pressed me on it. "It's no big deal."

"Except it's bothering you. I can tell. Talk to me."

Welcome home, Hudson. The two extremes between my mother and father were as stark now as they'd always been. One talked a lot, the other hardly at all. One wanted to know everything and anything about my life while the other was so busy running a school district I wasn't sure what he knew, unless he was displeased. Not that I had a bad relationship with my dad or anything. He was just . . . very different from Mom.

"Honestly, it's fine. I just know . . ." I hesitated. "The Encore thing will come up."

"Well, of course it will. Can you blame them?"

"No, I can't. But I hate having to be defensive about it."

"So don't."

It was all so simple for her. "I'm not embarrassed by it. Or any of my life choices."

"You know I support any choice you make. Not that I relish the idea of my son taking off his clothes for a living, but if it's what you want to do, then do it. But you can't expect Dominica's brothers to be thrilled by the idea."

"It makes people happy, Mom. That's all I want to do. There's so much shit in this world, is it so bad to want to put a smile on people's faces? I know I'm not solving world hunger or contributing to our future generations, like you and Dad . . ."

Mom took a sip of coffee and peered at me. But I had nothing else to say, really.

"Hudson. You were more emotionally honest with yourself at eighteen than your father is now. He works constantly, and hates his job more than he likes it, but never in a million years would he have considered quitting. You, on the other hand, figured yourself out much sooner than most people, and you know I'm proud of you, whatever you do."

"I know, Mom."

"Are you still content?"

"I don't know. I was."

"Not being ashamed of your job doesn't mean you have to do it forever. If Encore has run its course, so be it. If you decide a record deal isn't your life's dream, so be it. Things change. People change. But please don't ever become someone who does a job because they're too scared to quit."

"I won't, Mom," I said honestly. "But you're right. Things do change."

She smiled. "By change, do you mean they meet someone who makes them rethink their priorities?"

"You're getting ahead of yourself. We haven't even officially been on a real date."

She shrugged, unconcerned. "When you know, you know."

I sighed. “I wasn’t planning on talking about my life’s aspirations this early in the morning.”

“There’s no better time,” she teased. “Speaking of, you’re going back to Kitchi Falls after the wedding, right?”

“We are, on Monday. Why?”

“You have to stop by and visit your aunt and uncle. I told Dorothy you were in town.”

“No problem. How’s Rich?”

“Feeling fine, but honestly, I think he needs to slow down a bit. He’s had two health scares, and I worry about him.”

“Maybe they should think of retirement.”

“Are you kidding? And sell the shop? I can’t imagine it.”

“I can’t either,” I agreed. “Speaking of the shop, I have a new recipe for them. A bakery in Nashville makes well-known butter cookies. People line up and down the street for them.”

“And they just gave you their recipe?”

“I may have convinced one of the servers to give it to me.”

My mother, understanding the gist of my meaning, put up her hand. She didn’t want to hear any more. “They’ll be thrilled. But maybe don’t tell me any more about your methods.”

I laughed at her insinuation. “The girl is in college, Mom. It was nothing more than a little harmless flirting.”

Mom shook her head. “That’s good, I suppose.” She smiled. “Do you remember the time a waitress at that restaurant, I can’t remember the name, gave you ten dollars to flex your bicep for her and her friends?”

“I do. Can’t remember the name of it either.”

“I could hardly pull you out of the place, your head was so big.”

"If I remember correctly, she waited until you were in the bathroom to ask me."

"She did." Mom stood. "Another coffee?"

"Sure."

"I have a full day planned for us."

"Does it involve shopping?"

She made a face. "Of course not. I do want you to come home more often."

Feeling guilty about how little I'd seen my mom these past few years, I stood up and pulled her into me. My mother loved hugs, and I loved the look on her face whenever I gave her one without her asking.

"I love you, Mom," I said.

She didn't answer. Pretty sure it was because she was crying. So I squeezed a little bit tighter. It was good to be home. Especially when it brought me closer to seeing Min.

CHAPTER NINETEEN

dominica

So far, so good.

Aside from the fact that somehow, we'd forgotten a garter belt for Brooke, after a mad dash and literally four garter belts showing up in her hotel room, everything had gone off without a hitch thus far. Thursday we'd checked into Belhurst Castle and spent the day at a nearby spa. Last night at the rehearsal dinner we'd finally gotten to meet Brooke's mom, who was the spitting image of her daughter.

I tried not to let the fact that Hudson was less than an hour's drive from here distract me from the wedding. Thankfully, since last Wednesday, the topic hadn't come up again with my brothers. Mom and Dad only knew he was coming in from Nashville, but I'd avoided too many specifics so far. Thayle, on the other hand, was fit to burst with excitement. Not unlike me.

"Do you see him?"

The church was packed. Tina adjusted Brooke's train as the rest of us got into place to walk down the aisle. The church was decorated beautifully with roses to match our red bridesmaid's gowns, the Valentine's theme a perfect complement to the winter wedding, but with so many guests, it was impossible to find any one individual.

By the time the music started, my hands were shaking. He was here somewhere. Hudson had texted over an hour ago, saying he'd checked into Belhurst and was on his way to the church. Somewhere out there, he sat in a pew. I made my way down the aisle without tripping, even though my eyes constantly scanned the church.

But when I saw my brother's face, it suddenly became all I could focus on. Cosimo was looking past me, past all of us, waiting for Brooke. Watching him, I smiled when the moment arrived. When he first set eyes on his bride.

Do not cry. Do not cry.

I couldn't help it. The look on my brother's face, the fact that he reached up to wipe a tear from the corner of his eye. Crap. If I couldn't hold it in for a Clydesdale commercial, there was no way I could keep my eyes dry at the sight of my brother's expression right now.

After a few deep breaths, and a second or two staring at the ceiling, I got myself under control. The ceremony started, and I went back to pastime number one. Looking for Hudson. I'd been just about to give up when I saw him. Thankfully, I didn't faint.

He wore a navy suit and white shirt, no tie, looking like he'd stepped out of the pages of *GQ*. Gone were the hat and boots from our last meeting, unfortunately, but without them his classic good looks were on full display. When he smiled at me, and winked, I was surprised to still find myself standing.

The rest of the ceremony was a blur. With a tight turnaround to the reception so that guests didn't have to wait long since everyone was from out of town—even we locals were a half hour from home—there was a small window for pictures. Hudson already knew I'd be whisked off after the wedding, back to Belhurst Castle, and though the plan to meet me there seemed fine before, the extra hour dragged on now that it was actually here.

"One more of the whole family with cousins," my mother said, never one to pass up an opportunity for extended-family photos. It was nearly four o'clock already, and guests would begin to arrive for the cocktail hour soon. I'd told Hudson he could just meet me here at the hotel after the wedding was over, but he insisted on attending the wedding. Which was great, but knowing he was in town, so close, was making for the longest few hours of my life. I'd given Brooke and Cos my full attention, but now that it was almost time to see him. . .

"Are you dying?" Thayle asked as we broke away from the others getting photographed.

"You have no idea," I said. Then, on second thought, "Actually, you do."

Thayle had been my sounding board these past weeks.

"Just don't ruin your hair and makeup too badly," she said, knowing I was meeting Hudson in the lobby before the reception started. He had to get his stuff into the room, after all. Never mind that I technically could have left a key to the room for him at the front desk.

"Okay," the photographer said, "we're all set."

The woman from Belhurst who was organizing the reception took over. "We have about twenty minutes before cocktail hour. As you know, that will take place in the Meritage Ballroom. Since you're not doing a receiving line, you can freshen up and head in there anytime. Try to relax and enjoy yourselves, everything is all set and taken care of. When it comes time, and I begin to move guests into the Castle Ballroom, the wedding party and parents just stay put so we can announce you once everyone is seated. Any questions?"

Please don't let there be any questions. Thankfully, there weren't. I whispered to Thayle, "I'll be right back."

"Counting on it," she teased.

And then, finally, the moment I'd been waiting for. That I'd been dreaming of since we'd made these plans. Giving Thayle my bouquet—she took it without question—I made my way to the lobby.

There, leaning against the check-in counter, an overnight bag at his feet, was Hudson. I'd planned on being cool about the whole thing, but the second I saw him, I practically ran. His arms were open before I got to him. And then, as if we'd done it a hundred times, we embraced. I wanted to kiss him so badly, but we were surrounded by wedding guests checking in or just biding time before cocktail hour.

"You smell so good," I said into the crisp white shirt at his chest.

"You look so good," he said, pulling away to look at me. "My god, Min. You're absolutely gorgeous."

He should talk.

"Thank you. And so are you." I stepped back and nodded to his bag. "Ready to get settled?"

He leaned down, grabbed the bag, and whispered into my ear, "If by settled you mean kiss you senseless, then yes."

This man. Honestly, was he for real?

Taking the room key out of my purse, I led him through the lobby toward the main part of the castle where the guest rooms were located. "I can't believe you're here."

"Same."

When I looked back at him, Hudson smiled at me. Even

the man's teeth were perfect. Everything about him was perfect. "Do you have any faults at all?"

We turned a corner and then walked up to the second floor. I couldn't wait for him to see the view from our room. Scratch that, I couldn't wait to kiss him.

"Plenty. I can be pretty broody sometimes. As my mom says, I have high highs and low lows."

"I can't imagine that," I said.

"What about you? What do I need to know about Dominica Grado before getting in too deep here?" His tone was teasing, but as I opened our door, I suspected there was something more to it. As if he were serious about us getting, well, serious. Not that it was possible with the current state of affairs.

"Are you kidding me?" I asked, pushing the door open. "Where do I start? My brother Neo calls me a hurricane with no eye. Says the only time I'm calm is when I'm sleeping." We stepped inside. "Thayle actually says I'm always looking for the next 'thing' to keep busy because I'm afraid quiet time will make me anxious. Though I'm not sure that's true. I don't think I have any more anxiety than the next person. Just normal stuff."

The door closed.

"Let me help with any lingering anxiety you might be experiencing." Hudson dropped his bag, took my clutch from my hand, and tossed that too. Then quickly, I was back in his arms. His lips descended, capturing mine without words. Hudson's tongue dared me to return the intensity he offered, and I did. His hands cupped my cheeks as I gripped the arms of his suit coat for dear life. I simply couldn't get close enough to him.

When Hudson groaned, it was game over. I wanted so much more. But he pulled back.

"I think we have a wedding reception to get to. Not that I couldn't stay here all night with you in my arms," Hudson said.

I was falling in love with him.

There was simply no other explanation for how I felt at this exact moment. Had I ever actually been in love before? Because I'd never experienced such an all-consuming need to be with someone before. Some might say it was the long-distance situation, and that Hudson and I barely knew each other, but I did know myself. And this was simply not normal.

"I suppose you're right," I said, though neither one of us moved.

He kissed me again, this time less frantically. It was short, and sweet, his lips made for me. "It's good to see you in person, sunshine."

"Thanks for coming."

"My pleasure. And Mom already loves you for getting my ass home for a change. Her exact words."

"Well, I'm sure I'll love her too." And then, realizing I'd made an assumption about meeting her, I clarified, "I mean, if we meet. Not that we will but—"

"You will."

The obvious question hung between us. *Screw it. Take the bull by the horns, Min.*

"That implies this is more than a casual weekend." Holding my breath, I wondered if I'd just stepped over the line.

"I am about to meet your entire family after flying up here to see you. This is anything but a casual weekend."

Good point.

"To be clear, I have zero desire to date anyone other

than you." He really just said that. My heart raced. "Ever again."

I stared at him, flabbergasted. He didn't shrink from the words though. Hudson simply held my gaze and waited. He really was an extraordinary man in so many ways. Like he knew exactly what he wanted from life, never wavering.

"Me neither."

We were so far away from naked cowboys right now, it was insane. It was true, I'd been attracted to his looks. And okay, maybe his body too. But there was more to it, as crazy as that sounded even to my own mind. A pull, a draw? I didn't know.

"Then it's official," he said, letting go.

I reached down to grab my purse, and caught him staring at my backside when I stood. "You're not even trying to hide it."

His slow smile of appreciation was welcome, but also . . . we really did have to go.

"Sadly, we really have to go," I said.

"That's a shame," Hudson said, grabbing his duffle and walking farther into the room, "because it's a damn fine view."

I turned to look out the window. The lawn, covered in snow, led down to a lake. It was like a winter wonderland, not unlike the view from the Wine Cellar, which had picture windows that looked out onto a large deck and lawn, currently covered in snow, and beyond to the lake.

"It truly is beautiful," I said.

"Wasn't talking about the lake," he said, looking at me.

"Liar." I opened my purse and took out my lipstick, moving to stand in front of the mirror near the door. By the time I finished reapplying it, Hudson was behind me, also looking into the mirror. The look on his face would be frozen into my memory all night. He looked as if he would devour me, and I would gladly let him.

"So, when we go down there," I said, trying to sound casual. "I can introduce you as . . ." I hesitated. Despite our discussion, it still felt presumptuous.

Hudson continued to look at me in the mirror. "Your boyfriend?" he said, and I turned toward him. "I hope you do."

"A boyfriend who lives nine hundred miles away."

"Minor detail."

I laughed. "I mean, it's not really. But maybe something for another day's discussion."

"Exactly. Now let's head out before I kiss you again and force you to reapply your lipstick. Which I'm not sure I can survive twice."

"Oh, you like that, do you?" I teased.

"I like everything about you, Min."

He was so serious, I didn't laugh off the statement like I normally might have.

"Are we crazy?" I asked instead.

"Probably."

I shrugged. "Alrighty then, you ready to do this . . . boyfriend?"

"As ready as I'll ever be . . . girlfriend."

Hudson kissed me on the nose before we left the room. So far, our reunion had more than surpassed my expectations. Now, if my brothers behaved, it could prove to be the most perfect night, and the most perfect wedding reception ever.

CHAPTER TWENTY

hudson

Here went nothing.

We'd met Min's parents already. They'd been polite, though understandably distracted. Next up, apparently, was the bride and groom. Congratulating them both, I assumed Brooke and Min's brother Cosimo would be as equally distracted as they made their way through the room greeting guests.

"It's great to see you again," Brooke said.

"Same to you," I answered, pretending not to notice Cosimo—or Cos, as everyone apparently called him—glaring at me. "You look beautiful," I said truthfully.

"Thank you. Cos, say hello to Hudson."

I stuck out my hand, half expecting him not to take it given his expression. But he did, his grip firm. "We've heard a lot about you lately."

"Likewise. Min speaks highly of her whole family, but she seems to have a special affinity for her oldest brother." Though I only spoke the truth, it did seem to soften him ever so slightly.

"Because I'm her favorite," he said, letting go of my hand.

"I don't want to keep you from your guests," I said.

"Excuse me," Brooke said, stepping aside and hugging an older woman who approached her.

"You remember Thayle?" Min asked me as another man approached. "Though I'm not sure where she went. This is her fiancé, otherwise known as my brother Neo."

"Pleased to meet you," I said, extending my hand to him. He took it, thankfully.

"So you're the famous Hudson?"

"Famous?" I looked down at Min, who stood next to me. Her broad smile encouraged me to produce one of my own. I turned back to Neo. "I don't know about that."

"To some people you're famous," another voice behind me said. "The ladies in Nashville, at least."

Marco.

Min told me he was the most likely to give me trouble. According to her, he was the one "most likely to have an edge." Her prediction turned out to be right. But I wouldn't get into a pissing contest with the guy, and certainly not on her brother's wedding day. So I ignored the comment and reached out my hand for the third time in as many minutes, ignoring the fact that both Neo and Marco had swarmed us the minute Min and I started talking to Cosimo. They were trying to project strength, and I was fine with it. Not that she needed protecting, but if that was their goal, I wouldn't argue with it.

"You must be Marco," I said as he joined our huddle. Min swatted him on the arm, presumably because of the comment he made, as I waited for him to take my hand. For a second, I didn't think he would. But finally, reluctantly, he did.

His was the firmest grip of all.

"At your service," he said, though not entirely kindly.

"This is Hudson," Min said. "And if you aren't nice to him, there's going to be trouble." Her voice was teasing, mostly.

"Not on my wedding day," Cosimo said with the hint of a smile. "It looks like you have backup," he said to Min.

I turned just in time to catch Brooke's expression as she looked at her husband. It was a very clear signal to "be nice."

"It would be great if I didn't need it," Min said as I turned back to the group.

"I hope you don't blame us for being cautious," Neo said. "Given the circumstances."

"That's my cue." Cosimo nodded, a neutral gesture not at all hostile. Unlike Marco, who didn't bother hiding his contempt.

Saying goodbye to Cosimo, and hoping to nip this in the bud, I said to Min, "Would you mind grabbing me a beer? I'll be right there."

"And leave you with them?" She sounded appalled.

"I'll be fine," I said. Min hesitated.

"Give us some credit," Neo said to her. But still she dithered. I gave her a quick nod to tell her it was okay.

Clearly skeptical, she did walk away from us but continued to look back. I couldn't take my eyes off her. Until I remembered my companions.

"Not a wine drinker?" Neo asked. Since he was the vintner at Grado, admitting I didn't like wine was risky. But also the truth.

"I'm not," I said. "More of a beer guy."

"No worries," he said as Marco remained silent. "It's not

for everyone. Min said you grew up in Brookville, so I assume you still know your way around a winery."

"I did. And yeah, my parents are both big wine drinkers, so I've been to my fair share over the years. Just never really took to it."

"So," Marco finally spoke up. "You met Min at a strip club?"

Prepared for the attack, I didn't flinch. "I'm sure she told you I work for a male revue company. I sing and play guitar too. But yes, we met at my club."

"Nice," he sneered, not holding back.

"Marco," Neo warned.

"It's okay," I assured him. "I know I'm not the ideal candidate for a boyfriend for your sister, but it's just a job. I don't date customers."

"Except Min," Marco said.

"I rarely date customers," I amended.

"So just this once?" Marco asked.

"Alright, Marco, that's enough," Neo said. "I'm sorry he's being an ass. We're just looking out for Min."

"As I'd expect. But hopefully the fact that I'm here shows you that I'm serious about her."

"After spending one weekend together?" Marco struck again.

"I knew I shouldn't have left," Min said, handing me a beer.

"That was quick," I said. "Thanks."

"I think that's enough for now," she said. "The girls are all looking at us," she said of Brooke's friends who I'd met on the bachelorette trip. "They want to say hello."

"It was good to meet you all," I said, only partially lying. In fact, her brothers had been exactly as I'd expected—if not more good looking, and the Grado brothers were certainly that. If also a bit more prickly.

Marco said nothing. Neo nodded, the half-smile the best I'd get out of either of them for now.

"Were they horrible?" she asked as we walked away.

"They were exactly what I'd expect them to be. Protective." I took her hand, stopping us before we got to the others. "I can handle myself. Telling them to be nice isn't going to get any of your brothers to trust me. Hopefully that will happen in time, if they get to know me. For tonight, though, the only thing I want you to worry about is having a good time at your brother's wedding. Okay?"

She stood on her tippy-toes, and despite the fact that her brothers were likely still watching us, I'd never deny Min a kiss. Though I did make it a quick one. Too quick.

"I'm already having a good time," she said. "You're here."

"Honestly, Min, there's no place I'd rather be."

CHAPTER TWENTY-ONE

dominica

If only I were anywhere but here.

At the bar with Hudson. On the dance floor. In the bathroom helping Brooke lift up her wedding dress to pee. Literally anywhere else would be better than listening to Marco's date tell me every single detail about her new patient. Apparently, she was a nurse, which in and of itself was great. The fact that they basically ran the hospitals and knew more than just about anyone, including most often the doctors, made them heroes in my book. One of my aunts had been a nurse before retiring to teach part time in a local nursing school.

It wasn't that which was driving me crazy, but rather the fact that Marco had the balls to bust my chops and then stick me with a woman who refused to talk about anything other than her patients. I tried. In the half hour it had taken him to get a drink and then disappear to god knows where, knowing I wouldn't abandon her as the poor woman didn't know a soul, I tried to ask her other questions. Or talk about how beautiful the bride was. Or find out if she liked wine. But nope. The woman had a serious one-track mind.

Hudson looked back at me from the bar. He was talking to Neo, so I didn't want to call him over. At least one of my brothers was behaving around my boyfriend.

My boyfriend. That was so strange even to think in my head.

"Oh my goodness," my companion said suddenly. "Is that the bride and groom?"

Cosimo, apparently without warning, had scooped up Brooke and was now carrying her out of the ballroom. He was such a ham. Even though the reception was technically over, no one seemed to want to leave. The bartender had agreed to stay an extra hour, so this was essentially the after-party.

"It appears so," I said. The tip-off, I suppose, was that the woman being carried wore a wedding gown. "And look who finally returned."

"I'm so sorry," Marco said, rushing up to us. "A friend of mine just finished restoring—"

"Oh, these old cars," his date said. "Are you so sick of hearing about them?" she asked me.

As a matter of fact I was, but coming from her, it rubbed me the wrong way. But since I'd asked Marco to be nice, not that he'd held up his end of the bargain, I just smiled instead.

"Excuse me," I said, making my way to Hudson and Neo.

"What an exit," I said of Brooke and Cos.

Neo agreed. "Speaking of exits, have you seen Thayle?"

I looked around the room. "Not since we danced together a few songs ago."

"I'm gonna go find her. Talk to you guys later," he said, walking away.

"I'm so sorry to have left you hanging," Hudson said. "I

honestly only intended to grab a drink and come right back."

"No worries," I said, marveling at how good he looked in a suit. "I'm really glad you got a chance to talk to at least one of my brothers tonight."

"Neo seemed interested in my love of beer. He talked about Marco pushing to open an on-site brewery?"

"He's been talking about it for years. It's pretty much a go. We just have to break the news to my parents, who were really not keen on the idea."

"That's what he said."

"No, that's what *she* said." I smiled at my own joke.

"You're a nut. But," his tone lowered, "a really sexy nut. One I've been waiting all night to crack."

"That is literally the worst line in the history of pickup lines."

Hudson was already laughing with me. "Maybe because it's not a pickup line. More of a 'when can we ditch this party for one of our own' line."

"The bride and groom are gone, so . . ." I looked for my parents. They were nowhere to be found. The thought of making the rounds and spending the next twenty minutes saying goodbye to everyone . . . "Come with me."

Taking Hudson's hand, I wove us on the outer edge of the crowd so as not to be seen. We slipped out the side entrance, which took us into a hallway. I hiked up my dress and began to run. Hudson followed.

We hurried down a long corridor and into another, and then found ourselves woefully lost. But at least we'd escaped.

"This way," he said, somehow having a sense of where we were. He took us up a rear stairwell that opened to a block of rooms that did not appear to be in the main, newer section of the estate. The rooms were in the "castle," or the original building. Sure enough, though, a few more turns, and we ended up right at the elevator near the main lobby.

"I wish you liked wine," I said. "Check this out."

A cutout in the wall held a spout with small plastic tasting cups stacked beneath it. Grabbing a cup, I opened the spout and poured myself red wine.

"Look at that," he said, coming closer. "Free wine?"

"Yep. It's always filled too. Here, taste. It's a Chianti today."

He took a sip, made a face, and then gave the cup back to me. "I don't know how anyone could drink that stuff. No offense."

Finishing the wine, I headed to the room with Hudson next to me. Once inside, I flipped on the lamp, tossed my purse on the dresser, and immediately took off my shoes. I turned to Hudson as he was removing his jacket.

"Any chance you could help me with this dress?"

Hudson groaned. With a small smile, I turned my back to him, lifting my hair out of the way. I held my breath as he unzipped me. At the first touch of his lips on my neck, I closed my eyes. At the second, I actually held on to the dresser in front of me. I needed some stabilization, in more ways than one.

He trailed a path of kisses downward, slipping the dress off my shoulder, first one and then the other. I let the dress fall to the floor in a heap as I turned toward him.

Hudson looked down. "Oh my god, Dominica."

I reached for the first button of his white shirt. "You know, every time you've been naked in front of me . . ." I undid the second button, ". . . my hands have been tied behind my back."

"I'm sure I can find some makeshift cutoffs in a pinch."

His thumbs rubbed both of my shoulders as I continued to unbutton.

"No, thank you," I said, untucking Hudson's shirt from his pants. "I've been really wanting to do this." Now that he was fully unbuttoned, his shirt no longer a hindrance, I ran my hands over his abs. "I've seen many a six-pack in pictures but never actually touched one."

"Sunshine," he said, sliding off one of my bra straps, "you can touch mine anytime."

With both my shoulders now bare, Hudson leaned forward to kiss where the bra straps had been a second earlier. I'd half expected us to tear each other's clothes off the second we got in the room, but I liked this even more. His touch, his kisses, were deliberate, as if each one was precious.

Pushing his shirt off his shoulders, I tried to take it off but got snagged on the sleeves.

"Thanks for your help," I said as he finished the job. "I think it's only fair I follow suit." I reached back and unclasped my bra. Tossing it to the floor, I nearly came right then and there just watching his face.

And then he kissed me.

The slow undressing dance was done. His kiss was as hard and demanding as his hands. He cupped my breasts, rubbed both thumbs over my nipples, and even squeezed a bit. I pressed into him, wanting more.

He gave it.

Hudson trailed a path down to one breast, then after giving it the attention it deserved, he moved to the other. His teeth grazed me, just before he abruptly stopped. And dropped to his knees.

Hudson's stripper moves popped into my head as he then proceeded to remove my thong—with his teeth. Using the dresser behind me for support, I relished every touch, from Hudson's hand on my hip to his lips and tongue now exploring my inner thigh. When he stood and kissed me, I was so primed that it wasn't until I was already on the bed that I realized his intent.

Spreading my legs wide, he gave me one last look before the first touch of his tongue sent my hips into the air. Pressing them back down, he refused to let me move again, his hands pinning me exactly where I wanted to be pinned.

With every lick, I inched closer and closer. I pulled his head into me, circling and encouraging his movements, as if he needed it.

"I never came like this," I blurted, warning him.

Hudson looked up with an expression that could only have been described as determined. He actually chuckled then, and slipped first one finger, and then a second, inside me.

"Never?"

I swallowed. "Never."

"I'm so sorry," he said, his thumb now circling too.

I was about to ask Hudson what he was sorry for, exactly, but he replaced his thumb once again with his tongue, though his fingers remained in place. Incredibly, I began to tighten. As if sensing it, Hudson doubled down, and I didn't stand a chance.

Not that I wanted to.

"Hudson . . ." I did not hold back. Neither did he, his tongue some sort of miracle that needed its own insurance policy. Wave after wave took me, and by the time I returned to shore, I was pretty sure I needed a lifeboat.

"Holy hell," I said, having no other words to describe what had just happened.

"There's a first for everything," he said, smiling and clearly pleased.

Now it was his turn. And I was determined to make it just as good.

"You're right," I teased as I scrambled to sit up. "Like the first time you ride a Ferris wheel at the state fair or the first time you taste blueberry cheesecake ice cream. Which is my favorite, by the way." And for the coup de grâce: "And the first time you give your brand-new boyfriend a blow job."

It took a second for the words to sink in, and once they did Hudson adorably pretended as if he'd been struck in the chest. He fell to the bed as if dead, and I couldn't help but laugh. Thankfully, I knew one sure way to revive him.

CHAPTER TWENTY-TWO

hudson

I DIDN'T WANT THIS TO END. AS MIN WOKE UP FOR THE SECOND morning in my arms, I considered asking if she wanted to stay at Belhurst another night rather than spend the last two days of my visit at Grado. With the wedding guests leaving yesterday morning after the brunch, I had her all to myself.

And liked it this way.

Pulling my arms from under her head, I headed into the bathroom. By the time I was done, I thought for sure she'd have woken up. Then again, one of the things I'd learned about Min was that she could sleep through a tornado. Pulling on a pair of boxers, I opened the curtains just enough for a peek.

Looking out onto the lake, a familiar view from my childhood, I thought about how different the landscape was from my view in Nashville. I'd always wanted to live somewhere more exciting than Upstate New York, and I'd gotten my wish. Nashville was a fun town that I'd always enjoyed—until this trip.

Now, Nashville was the last place I wanted to be.

Turning back to Min, I was surprised to see her awake.

"Sorry about that," I said of the open curtain.

"Are you?" she teased.

As a matter of fact, I was not. I wanted her to wake up. To look at me. Talk to me. Tease me. Every moment with Min I felt more alive than I ever had onstage. More alive than I'd ever been.

"No," I admitted.

Before I could say more, she jumped out of bed and ran to the bathroom so quickly, I was sure something was wrong.

"You okay?" I called to her.

No answer. A few minutes later, she came out in a robe. "I really had to pee."

That was so on-brand for her. Even going to the bathroom was done with an unmatched zeal that sometimes made me dizzy. In a good way.

"Talk to me about that robe," I said, making my way toward her.

"Oh no, you don't. We have brunch reservations with Neo and Thayle back at the estate."

"I thought maybe you'd canceled," I said, reaching for her. Apparently, a new catering company in town had been courting Grado Valley. They were bringing a brunch to the Wine Barn as a sample of their fare. It had been booked before my visit was planned. Min had said she'd have taken today and tomorrow off, but as Grado's event coordinator, a supplementary role she took as seriously as her job running the Wine Barn, she felt obligated to be there.

"You know full well I couldn't cancel with our most-used breakfast and brunch caterer going out of business. I have a bridal shower in three weeks and might end up making all of the food myself if this doesn't work out."

I pulled Min toward me. "I'll help. I make a mean scrambled egg."

Kissing her, I marveled at how in sync we were with each other. Knowing we had to get going, but also not willing to let her go yet, I reached inside the fluffy white robe. Slipping my hand between Min's legs, noticing she was no longer arguing that we had to head to brunch, I slid one, and then two, fingers inside. Mimicking the movements of my tongue, I circled and pressed. Willed her to come for me.

Knowing she would.

These past two days, marred only temporarily by her brother Marco's relentless barbs at breakfast yesterday, had been nothing short of heaven. Knowing we'd not be having sex, I hadn't allowed myself to imagine slipping inside her.

Okay, maybe I'd imagined it a little.

But at this moment, I just wanted to put a smile on Min's face. And judging by the movement of her hips and the sounds she made, I was close. In fact, very close. She began to tighten around me, so I deepened the kiss even more.

I stopped kissing her long enough to say, "Come for me, sunshine."

And she did. I watched her face transform, burning her expression into my memory. Though I refused to dwell on the fact that I'd be leaving. Here and now was all that mattered.

She reached down between us, and I grabbed her hand to stop her. While I surely wanted to find my own release, I wanted something else more. For Min to know this wasn't about sex.

"Later," I said, hoping she didn't hear the strain in my voice. "For now, we've really got to get a move on."

“Who says that? ‘Get a move on’?”

“I do. Of course, if you’ve changed your mind about canceling . . .”

“Ugh.” Min all but stomped her feet as she tore away from me, clearly frustrated. I knew the feeling.

By the time we’d checked out and started driving back to Grado, I was starving. And not just for food. Holding Min’s hand in the car wasn’t enough. The need to be closer to her, to hold her in my arms, was frankly terrifying. Surely it had to do with the long-distance nature of our relationship, but never in my life had I wanted to be with someone more.

And she felt it too.

We’d lain in bed last night talking well into the morning. Knowing we were on the same page was good, but both of us acknowledged there were some tough discussions ahead.

“I don’t remember it being this big,” I said as she pulled up at the front of the estate. Since the winery was closed, we parked in a drop-off area. A massive archway with “GVV” engraved in the middle marked the official entrance to the estate.

“You can leave your stuff in the car. We’ll drive over to the cottage later.”

We got out and moved toward the entrance.

“So that’s the 1942 Wine Cellar,” she said, pointing to the largest building, on the right. “That’s the year my grandmother came to the U.S. Most of us just call it ‘the Cellar.’”

“It doesn’t look anything like a cellar.”

“There’s an actual cellar in it, but yeah, the tasting room and most of the offices are in there. It’s also where we make the wine. It’s been expanded a few times. The nicest part is the back deck, which leads down to the lake."

Behind us, where we'd driven in from, were the vineyards. In front of us, lay the main estate, as Min called it. And way down beyond an expansive, snow-covered field, I could see some of the cottages peeking through barren trees.

"The cottages are there," she said, pointing to the area I'd been looking at. "When it's nice, the lawn is where people set up chairs to listen to bands. It's a whole different vibe in the summer."

"I bet." We walked toward another building to our left.

"And this is my baby. The 1931 Wine Barn, named after the year my grandfather bought this land after emigrating from Italy. Actually, he bought a lot more of it, two hundred acres of grain farmland. All but sixty-five acres were sold during the recession."

"That's a shame." We walked up the stairs of what looked like a converted barn.

"It really is."

"So grain, huh?"

"Yep. In nineteen eighty-three, my parents, who always loved wine, went on a trip to Napa. They had the idea then to turn this into a vineyard, as if the area needed another one. After six years of research, they planted the first vines: chardonnay, riesling, pinot noir, and gewürztraminer. And here we are. Two wineries, twelve cottages, and a VIP boat tour later, I give you . . . Grado Valley Vineyards."

"You talk about it as if the vineyards are a family member. I love your passion for it."

She opened the front door of the Barn. I'd seen the inside before on a video call, but that hadn't done it justice. In the center of the main tasting room, a table was set. Her brother and Thayle were already sitting, and a woman who was obviously part of the catering team was just leaving them, heading into a back room.

"Sorry we're so late," Min said, looking at the server.

"The owner is in the back, finishing food prep," Thayle said. "Come sit."

Neo stood. I went to him, shook his hand, and then pulled a seat out for Min.

"How was Belhurst without the crowd?" Thayle asked, pouring two mimosas.

"Beautiful," Min said, sitting. "Just like the wedding."

"It was really nice." Thayle handed us the mimosas. "To a successful Grado wedding and the pleasure of your company," she said to me.

"Salute," all three said as we clinked glasses.

Neo didn't say much. I could tell he didn't like me, but at least he wasn't as obvious about it as his brother Marco. Min and I talked a lot about her brothers, especially Marco, and I knew this was going to take time.

"So how long are you staying?" Thayle asked me.

"My flight leaves Wednesday afternoon."

"Oh man, that sucks. You won't be here for family night?"

Neo caught my eye. Clearly, he was happy about that. But I at least had to try to win him over, so I addressed him. "I wish I was. I know how important it is."

"Family first," he said, finally speaking up. He started to say something else, but then he stopped, looking at Min, and never continued.

"Tell us about your family," Thayle said.

Min answered before he could. "You know his aunt Dorothy and uncle Rich. We're heading to the shop this afternoon."

"She's my dad's sister. He's from Kitchi Falls," I said.

"Would you ever move back here?" Neo asked, silencing the room. So much for subtleties.

"That's kind of a personal question, isn't it?" Min asked. Then to me, "You don't have to answer that."

"I don't mind," I said, having been thinking along the same lines. "It's complicated. I went down to Nashville to pursue a dream."

"So that's a no?" he pressed.

"Not necessarily. The dream has"—I looked at Min—"shifted a bit."

"How so?" Thayle asked.

"Like I told Min, I love writing songs and sharing my music, not that I do a ton of it down there since ninety percent of what I sing are covers. And maybe that's the problem. But maybe not. I just had a lot more fun doing it when it was a hobby and not a job."

"Like the ceramics," Min said to no one in particular.

"Oh god, the ceramics." Neo shook his head. "Those things were everywhere." Then to me, he explained, "Min made a bunch of ceramic knick-knacks at a summer sleep-away camp in sixth grade. She came back insisting ceramics was her new passion—"

"She had a lot of those," Thayle quipped.

"Until she got a part-time job at a ceramics place two years later. How long did you work there? A week?"

"It was at least three weeks," Min said. Then, taking note of Thayle's side-eye, she amended, "Maybe two. Point being, I get what you're saying."

Neo wasn't finished. "What would you do if you moved back? You've probably noticed a lack of male revues up here."

"Neo," Min warned, but I cut in. He hadn't said it maliciously.

"I got roped into that at a singing gig, and I'll admit the money is good. But it's not something I plan to do forever."

"Seems like it'd be hard to do that with a girlfriend," he added.

"Okay," Min said, "that's enough."

"Sorry about the delay." The caterer and his server came into the room, their arms laden with trays. Good timing.

Min reached over, squeezed my knee, and then stood, introducing herself and going into full-on business owner mode. I appreciated the gesture, but it wasn't necessary. I could hold my own with her brothers, even if I wished I didn't have to. I could count on one hand the number of people I'd known throughout my life who didn't like me.

On the other hand, this was the first time I'd dated anyone seriously since getting the job at Encore. I got it. The two things didn't mesh well, despite the fact that some guys could make it work.

Although, Min and I living so far apart didn't work all that well either, but coming back home for good would be a huge, life-changing move. Not one I was ready to take.

Yet.

CHAPTER TWENTY-THREE
dominica

"One thing I don't miss? Multiple feet of snow," Hudson said as we pulled up to the curb.

"I'm just glad the snow came before the wedding. I swear I became a meteorologist for a while there."

We got out of the car and headed to Devine Bakery. Hudson had promised to stop by the shop to see his aunt and uncle, and as much as I didn't want to share him, I really was excited for donuts. I usually limited myself to once a week, but this was a special occasion.

"Do you think you can get the recipe for their donuts?" I asked as we headed into the store.

"I think I could be persuaded to try."

Just before we walked in, Hudson grabbed my hand and pulled me toward him. I'd expected a quick kiss, but that didn't seem to be enough for either of us. His hand moved up my back and grabbed my neck as he pulled me even closer.

"Heads up," a male voice called, and Hudson and I broke off our kiss and turned to find Owen Smith approaching. "Brother number two is in the store."

Owen stopped in front of us. He and his family owned half of Kitchi Falls, including the general store next door.

"I'm not afraid of Marco," I said, smiling. Owen laughed, then looked pointedly at Hudson, prompting me to introduce the two men. "Owen, this is Hudson Parker, Dorothy and Rich's nephew. Hudson, Owen Smith."

The two men shook hands. "Heard you were in town," Owen said, to Hudson's surprise.

"You've been in Nashville too long," I said. "Up here everyone knows everything."

"Another thing I don't miss. Nice to meet you, Owen."

"Same to you. So, Min," he said to me, "Marco just told me about the brewery permit. Said to keep it on the down low?"

"Parents," I said by way of explanation. "We're planning on telling them this week."

Owen whistled. "Your dad is going to have a fit. But I'd say it's about time. We need some good beer at this end of the lake."

"We're pretty excited to break ground in the spring, if we can get everything in place."

"Good luck," he said. "See you around." Owen headed for the store.

Hudson opened the door of the shop. "Nice guy."

"He is." As we walked in, the smell of donuts and goodness greeted us. As did Hudson's aunt. She bolted up and ran around the counter. As the two embraced, I thought of the day Dorothy told me about him. I never could have imagined we'd be here now, Hudson at my side.

About to leave tomorrow.

We'd avoided talking about it until last night, but the only thing we'd accomplished was depressing each other with the thought. Staying in one of Grado's vacant cottages, we'd holed up for the night, sat by the fire and talked all night. Well, we did other things too, of course. And I'd come so close to letting myself go completely. If there was anyone I wanted to lose my virginity to, it was Hudson Parker.

But something held me back.

That something was related to Dorothy chastising him for not coming back in so long. Hudson's life wasn't here, in Kitchi Falls, or even in Brookville across the lake where he was raised. His life was in Nashville, and mine would always be at Grado. Two facts that didn't jibe very well.

When a customer walked in, Dorothy moved back behind the counter and told us to sit down. Planting ourselves on two stools at the side counter near the check-out, we waited until the customer finished placing their order.

"Let me guess," Dorothy said as she reached beneath the counter, "cinnamon donut and a coffee?"

She knew me well. I nodded.

"I'll have the same." Hudson smiled at me as Dorothy prepared the coffees.

"I hear your mom was thrilled to have you home," Dorothy said.

"How did you hear that?" he asked, and I wondered if Hudson knew anything about his aunt. Dorothy was the town gossip. If she didn't know about something, it likely didn't happen.

"She called me yesterday, and asked if you'd stopped by," she said, giving us the coffees and a plateful of donuts. I was totally screwed. No way I could stop at one.

"Min and I just got in yesterday from Belhurst. We're sorry you couldn't make the wedding."

"Your uncle is doing better today," she said. "He's just had a rough time of it lately."

Poor Rich had been in and out of the hospital three times in as many months. It worried Thayle, who lived next door to him and Dorothy. Rich was like a grandfather to her.

"We're headed there next," Hudson said.

As he and his aunt caught up, I stayed mostly quiet, watching him. This guy was so far removed from the male dancer who had tied my hands behind my back, twice. That man was incredibly sexy, of course. But this one, with his jeans and sweater and navy Patagonia coat, sitting casually next to me chatting with his aunt, in some ways, was even hotter. Maybe just because he was here, in my hometown. And I so desperately wanted him to stay.

"I'm sorry you have to leave already tomorrow," Dorothy said.

Ugh, just what I didn't want to think about.

"I am too," Hudson said, looking at me.

This sucked.

"Then stay and work here," Dorothy blurted. "We could use the help."

Dorothy's words hung in the air, no one saying anything for a second until she laughed. "I'm just teasing you. I know working at a bakeshop isn't exactly your life's dream. But we could use you here."

"Do you think it's time to consider selling?" Hudson asked.

Why was I disappointed? Of course he wasn't going to say, *Yes, Aunt Dorothy, I'd love to give up my singing career and come work in a bakeshop*. But that would've been nice.

"I would sell in a heartbeat. But talk to your uncle. He's the stubborn one."

"I will," Hudson said, the concern in his voice evident.

Another customer came into the shop, and Dorothy was momentarily distracted.

"A perfect solution," I teased him. "Move back home, work for your aunt and uncle and"—I waved my hands as if doing a magic spell—"ta-da! All of our problems are solved."

Instead of laughing at my joke, Hudson looked me in the eyes, so seriously that it worried me a little.

"Would you want me to come back here, Min?"

My hand froze halfway to my mouth, the coffee I held forgotten. Was he serious? Was that a serious question? "Of course I would."

"We haven't known each other for very long."

I didn't miss a beat. "Doesn't matter. When you know, you know."

I'd never held anything back from Hudson, never played games with him, and I wouldn't start now.

"You kids look so serious all of a sudden. What are you chatting about over there?" Dorothy asked.

The moment was gone. But there was no denying it had been a moment.

"Nothing," Hudson said evasively as the customer thanked Dorothy for the baked goods.

"Stay safe," she called to him.

"Are we getting some bad weather?" I asked.

Dorothy's jaw dropped as she focused back on us. "Have the two of you been living in a cave? Big storm tomorrow."

Hudson and I exchanged a glance. Indeed, we sort of had been living in a cave these past few days.

"How much?" he asked. It seemed you couldn't take the Northeast out of a guy. He knew the right question for sure.

"They're saying up to two feet."

"Ah shit," he muttered, then apologized. "Sorry, Aunt Dorothy."

Then Hudson looked at me. I already knew what he was going to say.

"You have to be back for Thursday?" I asked.

"I have so many shifts to cover," he confirmed. Then to Dorothy, "To get a week off, I had to move things around quite a bit. I'm working Thursday through Tuesday straight, one job to the next."

She frowned, her disapproval obvious. Which, frankly, was kind of annoying. The guy was a dancer, not a hit man for the mob for god's sakes. "Well, you're not getting out tomorrow, that's for sure."

For a second, my heart skipped at the possibility of Hudson staying. But given the panicked look on his face, I realized the opposite was true.

"No," I said quietly. "Don't say it."

To be fair, at least he looked as devastated as I felt. "I'm sorry, Min."

He obviously meant it.

"Excuse me," he said, pulling out his phone. "I have to call the airline, see if I can get out ahead of the storm."

Dammit. Part of me hoped he couldn't get out, which was extremely uncharitable. I knew how many favors he'd had to secure to get up here, and Hudson wasn't the kind of guy who shirked his duties.

But still, it sucked. Really, really sucked.

I reached for a second donut.

CHAPTER TWENTY-FOUR

hudson

"I'm so sorry."

I must have said it twenty times already, and I'd meant it every time. We stood in the front room of the cottage, our temporary haven against this very thing. Leaving Min was always going to happen, but having another twenty-four hours would have been nice.

Though it might not have made a difference. Bottom line was, we lived two different lives. Her brother, who we'd run into just before leaving the bakeshop, had been spot on with his comments. I'd thought Min would kill Marco when he had said, "Oh, you have to leave early. So sorry about that," with a tone that made clear he was anything but sorry. At the risk of pissing off someone Min loved dearly, I had stepped in. But telling him that he was out of line had only succeeded in making his sister feel bad and definitely hadn't earned me the good standing I'd been hoping for when meeting her family.

But even as I'd protested Marco's comments, I knew he had a good reason for feeling the way he did. Seeing

Dominica in her environment had made it pretty clear that her world and mine were not compatible.

"I know," she said, looking at my luggage. "Me too. I feel like we were just getting started."

"Come here." I pulled her to me. Kissing Min had become so natural, it was a wonder we hadn't been doing it for years. I refused to let her go. She held on to my jacket for dear life, and I did the same. This felt more like the end than it did goodbye for now.

"Maybe I can come down to you soon." Her eyes searched mine.

"I'd like that," I said honestly. "It will be hard for me to get away again any time soon."

"It's easier for me now in the winter, but once the spring hits . . ." She trailed off.

"You'll be crazy busy," I finished for her.

She didn't deny it.

I had less than ten minutes before I risked not getting to the airport in time to catch my rescheduled flight. "What are we doing here, Min?"

"Don't ask me that," she said, not letting go. "Anything but that."

"Because you know . . ." I couldn't say it. Our lives existed in two different places. "I don't have the answers," I said honestly. "I don't even know what I want next. Besides you, of course."

"I guess you need to figure that out before we can really have this talk," she said. "At least you got to see your aunt and uncle before you left."

After leaving the shop, we'd been able to visit with my uncle, who seemed to be having a good day. But by the time we got back to the cottage, there hadn't been time to do much more than pack.

"And lucky enough to nab a seat on a flight tonight."

She scoffed. "Yeah, super lucky. I'm so glad there was a seat."

"I feel like you're being facetious," I teased.

"Me? Not at all."

If I really wanted to be charitable with Min, to do the right thing, I should let her go. Let her date other guys, live her life. But the idea of it was so repugnant, I just couldn't do it. One thing I could do, something that I'd been thinking about all week, was possible though.

"If it's any consolation, after I cover for the guys who took my shift for the last week, I'm done dancing."

Min pulled back to look me up and down, as if seeing more of me might illuminate my words. I had thought to tell her tonight, in bed, in a different way. But this would have to do.

"Are you serious?" she asked.

"I am. It's been a lot of fun, and I love those guys. But if we're going to be together, it's not right."

"Is this because of my dick brother?"

Marco was a dick, but I wouldn't confirm it to her. "It's not."

"What about the money?"

"I can easily pick up some extra gigs, a bartending shift or two if I need it. Working with Encore was never going to be forever. It just feels like the right time to quit."

"Are you one hundred percent sure?"

I took her in my arms again, knowing it was time.

"I'm sure," I said, squeezing her so tightly I was afraid I might hurt her. But Min squeezed back just as hard. After a final kiss, I picked up my duffle and suit bag.

"Thank you."

It looked like she wanted to say more. I know I did. But

when Min stayed silent, I did too. It was just too soon for those words. And also, despite the fact that I was giving up my most lucrative job as a way to show Min I was committed to her, it also felt rather futile. As if telling Min I loved her would only make it harder when we couldn't find a way to be together for more than just a few days.

"You're welcome," I said, wanting to pull her back into my arms. Wanting to make love to her more desperately than I'd ever wanted anything in my life. Wanting to stay. Wanting to tell her how I felt.

But I did none of those things. I had to get to the airport. And Min had to get back to her life without me. Back to a family who despised me. Back to a world it seemed less and less likely I'd ever be a part of. So instead, I smiled.

And then I left.

CHAPTER TWENTY-FIVE

dominica

"HEY, YOU," I SAID.

Thayle plopped on a stool at the bar. We were closed today, so I could have easily worked from home. But being in the Barn felt more like home than anywhere, even more than the house where I grew up. Lately, it felt as if the time may have come for me to move out. I still adored Mom's cooking, and I knew she would be really sad to see me, the last of her "babies," leave, even if I, like my brothers, only moved to an estate cottage a short drive from them. It was time, though.

"I won't ask what's wrong since I already know," she said.

I closed my laptop. After hiring the new catering company, we'd booked two brunch events thanks to Brooke's master marketing, but I didn't have the heart to look over the details this very moment. Both events needed to be fleshed out by the end of the week.

"It's not like me not to want to work."

"No," Thayle said. "It's not. I thought you'd be excited about the trip, at least."

It had been nearly a month since Hudson left, and yeah, I was excited to see him next weekend. Beyond excited. Still . . .

"I am, obviously."

Thayle laughed. "You look it."

"I was just thinking about moving out. That maybe it's time to get my own place."

"And that's what has you bummed?"

I shrugged. "I don't know."

Thayle was quiet. I could tell she was weighing whether or not to say something.

"Go for it," I told her. "Say what's on your mind." She really was the sister I never had.

"Moving out means thinking about next steps. Your future."

That was all she said. But it was enough. "I guess. And I'm so excited to see Hudson I could burst. But then what? I come back here, get a place—"

"One of the cottages?"

"Probably. Although that's one more we can't rent out."

"That's always been residual income for the estate. With Neo's rating and Brooke's brilliant marketing, Grado is as well-positioned as it has been in years."

She was right, of course. So much for Cos's worry about taking over. Since our parents retired, we'd had one win after another, with ventures like the addition of a dock and VIP tour—Brooke's idea—working out even better than anticipated. The icing on the cake had been a starred review of one of Neo's newer wines, which took our success to a whole new level. It had been a phenomenal run so far.

"I know. Although I'm not sure living that close to Marco is a good idea."

"You see him a hundred times a week already," she said.

"True. And I do love him but . . ." There was no need to finish. Everyone knew Marco and I had not spoken for days after Hudson left. The one thing I'd asked him to do, not to be a dick to Hudson, and he couldn't manage even that small request. I didn't buy the "I'm just looking out for my sister" crap. Even if true, that didn't excuse his behavior. Not that Cos or Neo were jumping for joy at the idea of my long-distance relationship, but at least they hadn't been outright rude to Hudson.

"Well, you'll see Hudson soon. You can talk about it then."

"That's the problem. What's there to talk about? I'm here. He's there. Just two nights ago Ray Spencer came out to hear him sing. Yesterday Bruce—the club owner who set it all up—called Hudson to say Ray liked what he heard. He thinks a recording offer might be a serious possibility."

"Ahhh, now I get it."

I rushed to add, "I'm so happy for him. Really, I am."

"Of course you are. But you can also be sad for yourself at the same time."

I was just going to say it out loud. "Because if he signs a record deal, it's game over for us."

"You'll never leave Grado."

That hardly deserved a response, and Thayle knew it. But I'd give one anyway. "This place is my life. My family is here. This winery"—I gestured to the Barn my mother and I had basically built from scratch—"is everything to me. A celebration of the women in our family, a perfect place for girls to have fun with their friends, to come together to enjoy each other, and friendship. To enjoy life. It's not just a bunch of wine bottles." I stopped. "I'm sorry," I said, having gotten overly passionate. "You know that better than anyone. You see what Neo goes through to make this wine."

"Which is how I know you'd never leave. Not even for a man you love."

She waited for me to deny it. I didn't, of course.

"I was going to do it that night." I'd not told anyone this before, not even Thayle. It didn't matter after he'd left. But now that I was heading back to Nashville for a weekend, I'd been thinking nonstop about it.

"You were going to give him your virginity?"

I nodded. "I planned to next weekend."

"Planned? As in, past tense?"

"I don't know what to think. It seems just as likely I might never see him again as it does that he's the one for me. Actually, more likely."

"You've always said it was more out of habit than intention that you stayed a virgin for so long."

"Which is true. But now it's like, I don't know, stopping on mile twenty-five of a marathon."

"Ugh, can you imagine running twenty-six miles?"

"Not in a million years."

"But I suppose if you ran twenty-five, that final mile wouldn't be so bad."

"What are we even talking about now?" I laughed at Thayle's expression, the thought of running so far making her visibly pale. "Enough gloom and doom. Did you eat lunch yet?"

"Actually, no. I came in to see if you wanted to take a break, go try that new deli that opened up in town."

"I've been wanting to check it out. Imagine, something new in Kitchi Falls."

"It's a miracle, for sure."

"And we won't talk about Hudson for the entire lunch." I stood up and grabbed my laptop.

"If you want. Or we can the whole time. Up to you."

I was so grateful for Thayle, for my best friend and soon-to-be sister-in-law. Actually, I had a lot to be grateful for. So why did I still feel like I wanted to crawl back into bed and not come out for a month? Hibernate until spring and when I woke up, it wouldn't feel like my heart was being ripped from my chest every time I thought about the inevitable. We were only delaying it, pretending everything was fine. But ultimately, it wasn't. I'd fallen in love with a man who was currently singing country songs in his sexy jeans and sexy flannel to wide-eyed adoring women at a honky-tonk in Nashville while I froze to death in the freaking tundra up here in New York.

Thayle and I grabbed our purses, and that was when I smelled smoke.

CHAPTER TWENTY-SIX

hudson

"Sounding good, Parker."

I started to pack up as Jeff and his band made their way to the stage. The first time I played down here, it had seemed so big. So many honky-tonks, so many bands. I'd wondered how anyone could possibly "make it" with all the talent that seemed to ooze out of the very pores of the city. But gradually, the community had revealed itself to me. The more I'd played, connected, learned . . . it had become smaller. Supportive and competitive at the same time.

It was a community I'd grown to love.

"Thanks, Jeff. Relieving me again?"

"Looks like it," Jeff said as I jumped down from the stage. "Heard you played for Ray Spencer this weekend at Robert's?"

"That made the rounds pretty quick," I said, nodding hello to Jeff's bandmates.

"You know how it is."

"Sure do."

"Have you heard anything yet?"

"No," I said. "Bruce set up the gig and he seems to think Ray was impressed."

Jeff's brows drew together. His gray hair and beard and the wrinkles around his eyes were a testament to his longevity in this town. His astuteness was no surprise.

"Why do you make it sound like that's not great news?"

I didn't mince words. "Remember the girl I mentioned?"

"The one you met from the bachelorette party?" Before I could say any more, he whistled. "Someone has it bad."

"You could say that. Problem is, she's part owner of a family winery back home in New York."

"Which means she's not going anywhere."

"Right."

"And you might be. If Ray Spencer has ears, anyway."

I hadn't meant to make this a therapy session. But Jeff had always been so easy to talk to. "Thanks man, I appreciate that." Then I asked a potentially rude question. "Did you guys ever pursue a deal?"

He grunted. "Back in the day, sure. But then we got wives and families and side gigs. This is enough for us. We stopped chasing and started living."

I slung my guitar case around my shoulder, took out my wallet and slipped a twenty into their tip jar. "For a round," I say. "Have a great set, and thanks for the advice."

"Can't say I gave you much of it. Good luck with Ray."

I wasn't sure Ray was who I needed luck with most, but I thanked him and headed to the bar to tip the bartender. Instead, I found myself ordering a drink, propping my guitar up and positioning myself facing the stage. I hadn't seen these guys play in a long time, and if there was any compliment you could pay a musician, it was listening to their music. So I did And reminded myself what made me love this city in the first place.

We were starting to get more warm days than cool ones and the windows were open today. The streets, even though it was dinnertime, were already packed with people. They streamed into the bars, smiled, laughed, clapped along to the music, drank beer or whiskey or whatever their poison, and lived life. It was such a great fucking thing, the ability to let it all go even if just for a song or a day or a weekend.

Good for them.

When my phone buzzed, I almost didn't reach for it. It had been a long time since I let myself just enjoy the music without thinking so hard about what to do next. When I saw the text though, all of that was instantly sucked into a black hole of unimportance. My heart raced as I scanned the message again.

Hi Hudson. It's Thayle. Can you give me a call? It's about Min. She's not hurt.

I ran out of the bar so quickly, it was only as I slammed into a tourist that I realized my guitar was still inside. I didn't even care. My hand shook as the phone rang.

"Hello?"

I thought for a second it might be Min's voice, but it wasn't.

"Thayle? What the hell is going on?"

She took a deep breath. "The Wine Barn. It's gone."

"Are you okay?"

The man sitting next to me on the plane to me reminded me of my dad. He had the same gray hair around his temples, the same build, and probably could have passed for his brother. The minute he sat down, I'd felt a strange affinity toward him, as you might with someone who looks like a friend or family member. I hadn't said anything, though. He also looked like the kind of guy who wanted to be left alone. Since takeoff, he hadn't removed his earbuds until now.

Oddly, I wasn't looking at him when he asked the question. But as I turned to him now, the clouds speeding past as our plane headed north, he gave me his full attention.

The polite thing to do would be to say yes. A stranger didn't need to be burdened with my problems. And yet, his kind eyes prompted me to offer the truth.

"Not completely," I found myself saying. "But I will be."

He folded the magazine on his lap. "Fear of flying?"

"Nah. I figure if it's my time, it's my time. You?"

He laughed. "I hope not. I'm a pilot."

"Sitting back here in coach?"

"Courtesy flight. Unplanned trip back home."

"Rochester?"

"Just outside of it. You?"

"I'm originally from Brookville but moved to Nashville a few years ago."

"No shit? I've been there a few times. Grado's a legend on Seneca."

"I've been there. Nice place."

"Beautiful," I remarked. "A fire destroyed the Wine Barn, one of the wineries on the property."

"Oh man, that's awful."

That wasn't even the half of it. "My girlfriend actually ran the Wine Barn. It meant a lot to her. Min has been building the place up for years."

"I'm sorry to hear that."

"Thanks," I said weakly, worried I was burdening this guy with my personal issues. When the fire department had said the Barn couldn't be saved, Min had gone home. She'd refused to go back to the estate. To say she was devastated was an understatement. What scared me most was the fact that Marco had suggested she call me. I could only imagine the state she'd been in for him to even consider such a thing.

"No one was hurt?"

I shook my head. "No, thank god. But my girlfriend is . . . taking it hard."

"I can imagine. I'm sure she'll be happy to have you there."

I hoped so.

"I haven't talked to her since it happened," I said. "She ran out of the building without her phone and hasn't gotten a new one yet." At least, I assumed she hadn't. Since Thayle called, there had been no word at all. I'd caught the first flight out and hadn't looked back.

"Have you been in touch with her family?"

Talking to this pilot was like talking to an understanding version of my father. One who wasn't disappointed I'd "wasted" my education degree. The resemblance really was remarkable.

"I haven't. We only met once, and honestly her brothers don't care for me much." I told him about my profession, meeting Min, the wedding. And then, realizing I was oversharing with a complete stranger, I cut off abruptly. "Sorry to unload all this on you. Honestly, things could be much worse. That Min and her family are safe are all that matters."

"Yes, of course." He nodded with an understanding smile, then stuck out his hand. "Name's Barry, by the way."

His handshake was firm, his eyes crinkled from smiling.

"Same to you," I said.

When he dropped his hand, Barry resettled himself in his seat and said, "I was an accountant for twenty-five years. Hated Mondays. Hated the job. And most of all, hated my boss. lived for the weekends, and for my two kids. My oldest son got me flying lessons six years ago for Father's Day. It's something I always wanted to do but I never had any time." He smiled. "But here we are. Second career. A new lease on life." He sighed. "I wish I had words of wisdom for you other than to follow your heart. Don't make the same mistake as me, getting pigeonholed into something you think you should be. Though, you don't seem to be the type to do that."

I thought of my father. Of the fight we had just before I left for the wedding. "No, I'm not."

"So tell me about your girlfriend."

We spoke for the rest of the flight. Though I never did tell Barry he looked like my father. I did thank him for distracting me, but now, as the blast of frigid air assaulted me when the sliding doors of the airport opened, it all came back. It was all I could do to keep moving forward as I imagined Min's devastation over the fire. But I reminded myself of the decision I'd made the moment Thayle first texted me, worried about her.

No regrets, Hudson.

It was a motto I'd sworn by, and one I was determined to stick to. Even now.

CHAPTER TWENTY-SEVEN

dominica

"Sweetie—"

I held up a hand, cutting my dad off. "I can't, Dad. Not yet."

He and my mother had just come home from the estate. Mom was in the tub, and Dad and I sat at the kitchen counter, like we'd done a thousand times before. Only tonight, neither of us smiled. He wasn't cracking corny jokes. The mood was as it should be, somber and depressing.

My beloved Barn was gone.

Technically, it was all of ours. But I'd redecorated it from the top down. Put so much TLC into that building that it had become more than a second home for me. It was a part of me. Now all of it was gone.

"I hate seeing you like this."

"And I hate adding to your stress. But I just can't go back to see it yet."

He sighed. "I understand it's hard."

"I feel like I'm about to crawl out of my skin," I

explained. "I actually got in the car this afternoon to go see it, but I couldn't do it. How could it be completely gone?"

"We will rebuild, Min. No one was hurt, and that's all that matters."

I swirled the wine in my glass over and over again. Dad had poured us two glasses when he came home. For our family, wine meant comfort. It was predictable and familiar. It gave our family purpose. A common goal that bound us together. But right now, it was also a reminder that when I did go to the estate, the Wine Barn would be nothing but rubble and ashes.

"It burned so quickly."

"It was old," he said, repeating what the fire chief had told him. "There was nothing they could do."

Ironically, we never even saw the initial flames. The smell of smoke alone had us running from the building. I hadn't even brought my phone outside, so Thayle called 911. By then we could see flames from the back of the building, near the courtyard. We'd watched in disbelief as the fire quickly spread to the front of the building.

The rest of it was a blur. My brothers had come, one by one. The sirens had announced what I'd thought would be our saving grace. We'd watched in horror as they put out the flames only to reveal a shell of a building, most of the Barn simply . . . gone. From shock to disbelief, then anger and now sadness, it had been a roller coaster of emotions, ones I wasn't quite ready to face. So, unlike the rest of my family, I'd come home and hadn't returned yet. Cos was dealing with the insurance company, so there was no reason for me to be there.

Thayle had been a godsend. While I'd been paralyzed into sitting here, in my kitchen, she'd texted Hudson to let him know what happened, and that I currently had no phone. Or laptop. Thankfully, being winter, there were only two upcoming events at the Barn, both of which Thayle had already moved to the Wine Cellar.

"The wine," I said, thinking of how much we had stocked. "The brand new furniture."

"Min." My father grabbed my hand. "Min," he repeated.

I looked at him, tears blurring my vision. "I'm being silly, I know. We're safe," I repeated, angry with myself for not being able to pull it together.

"You're not being silly. The Wine Barn was yours, and just like that, it went up in flames. Literally. You need time to grieve."

I wiped my eyes with one hand, still holding my father's hand with the other.

"What is it, sweetie? Tell me."

I hated self-pity but couldn't stop myself. "I have nothing," I said, hating the words as they flew from my mouth, knowing they weren't true. I had my family, and that was what mattered. But I still couldn't help it. "No Wine Barn. No Hudson."

Dad's eyes softened. "You broke up?"

"No. But we might as well have. He's in Nashville. I'm here. It's never going to work."

"You love him." It wasn't a question, and I didn't need to answer. "You don't talk about him much to us."

I sighed. "I've already got the boys on my back. Especially Marco. They don't agree with his lifestyle, even though he's stopped dancing. I just assumed you'd feel the same way."

Dad squeezed my hand. "At least give me a chance to have an opinion, Min."

He pulled his hand from mine, reached for the wine bottle, and refilled his glass with Brooke Blend. One of the

Barn's wines. So many of them were lost in the fire. I was almost glad my laptop had burnt to a crisp. I wouldn't have to look at the inventory of what we'd lost.

Which was beyond silly because of course I would have to do it eventually.

"Hudson seems like a good guy, and that's all I ask for. Someone who makes you happy and treats you well. The rest is secondary. Like the Barn. When we started Grado Valley Vineyards, it was nothing but a dream, a few vines, a card table, and a cash register. What we've been able to do over the years, what you and your brothers have done since we retired, is nothing short of remarkable. You know as well as I do, it's our family that makes Grado special. Not the buildings. Just us, and the wine."

"You're right, of course."

"You'll come down in the morning? I think it's important for you to be there. To begin to heal."

I shrugged. Despite the pep talk, I wasn't sure I was ready.

Already on edge, I nearly jumped out of my skin at the knock. Dad and I exchanged a look. Who could possibly be at the front door at ten at night? Anyone who would be coming now should be able to just walk right in.

"I got it," Mom called. That was a quick bath for her.

Dad looked over my shoulder. I spun around to do the same, curious and ready to go see who it was. But I didn't need to get up. Standing in the doorway, filling its frame, was Hudson.

And he was wearing a cowboy hat.

CHAPTER TWENTY-EIGHT

hudson

I KNEW THE MINUTE SHE LEAPED INTO MY ARMS.

To be fair, I probably knew before that. But holding Min after seeing her face, I knew for certain that I loved her.

As she sobbed into my shoulder, I pulled her hair aside and held her close. Her father smiled, and with a brief nod of approval, he placed his hand on my back and moved past us. I hadn't even set my duffle down yet, but I'd have stood there all night if she wanted.

"What are you doing here?"

When Min pulled away, her face streaked with tears, I was too overwhelmed to answer. Instead, I dropped my bag and kissed her. Hopefully her parents weren't still in the vicinity because the welcome kiss turned into something more, and pretty damn quickly.

As it deepened, the distance between us now completely closed, I never considered stopping. Unfortunately, she did eventually, repeating her question.

"What are you doing here?"

"Thayle told me about the fire, so I got the first flight

out." Holding her in my arms felt as good as I'd remembered. "Are you okay?"

I could see she wasn't. Min's eyes started to tear up again. So I kissed her again. I knew I couldn't permanently take away the pain, but for now . . .

It was a while before we found ourselves sitting at the kitchen counter. Unsurprisingly, with two red wines in front of us.

"Oh shit, I forgot. You don't like wine."

"It's fine," I said. "It's time for me to get on board. Can't date a vineyard owner and not like the stuff." I took a sip. Really, I did not like the stuff. But I pretended it was okay as it seemed to make Min happy that I tried. "Tell me what happened."

As Min explained how old, faulty wiring had caused a small fire that turned quickly into an inferno that swallowed the 1931 Wine Barn, my head spun with plans. And questions. Did I tell her tonight? No, it wasn't the time. She needed to get this out first.

"I haven't been back down there yet."

"All day?"

She nodded. "I couldn't make myself do it. Tomorrow I planned to get a new laptop and phone but . . ."

"But you weren't planning to go to the estate."

She shook her head. "My dad thinks I should. For closure. But I just don't want to see it."

"I understand," I said, trying to. "But I agree with him. It'll only eat you up inside, and you have to go down there eventually."

She blinked. Despondent.

"You're always looking ahead, Min. And I do think living in the moment is better than worrying about the future, but I also know that's not completely you. I've never met anyone who loves life like you do. Who plans for the next day, or adventure, with the same zeal as you. If this tragedy forces you to slow down, it's probably uncomfortable for a reason. But I also know you won't stay down for long. Might as well embrace who you are and just dig right in."

"How could you know all that? How could you know me so well, better than some of my brothers even?"

I winced at the mention of her brothers, and she laughed. "It's what you do," I said, forging ahead. "You listen and get to know the people you love."

Min's eyes widened.

"I love you, Dominica. So fucking much."

"You are so romantic," she said, looking at the hat that now sat on the counter between us. I'd worn it to make her laugh. To cheer her up. Min looked up at me. "I love you too. I really do. But what does that even mean for us? How long are you here?"

"We'll see," I said, evasively. "I have to make some calls in the morning."

"I can't imagine how you got time off again."

"Don't worry about that now. I'm here for you. Just worry about rebuilding. Getting down to the estate and digging in."

She frowned. "Marco said he could have the builder down there tomorrow. I told him I wasn't ready."

I didn't want to pressure her. This was her decision. "It's up to you. Either way, I'll be here."

She jumped from the stool and came around to me. I held her to me, trying to ignore the press of her breasts against my chest. Trying to pretend I wasn't having dirty thoughts of Min, seeing as this was anything but the appropriate time. Or place.

Min needed something else right now.

"Okay," she whispered into the crook of my neck. "We'll do it. Marco will be thrilled."

Marco.

If nothing else, the reminder splashed cold water on my randy thoughts of a woman who was now whispering "I love you so much" into my ear. But that problem, and the more serious issue that Min and I needed to discuss, could wait until morning.

CHAPTER TWENTY-NINE

dominica

It was worse than I'd imagined.

We'd closed Grado for the week, so thankfully no one was there to see it but us. Hudson and I walked under the GVV sign hanging overheard and headed toward the scorched earth. We'd yet to see anyone else, though I knew my brothers were on the estate. I still didn't have a phone, but Mom had told me the boys were all down here already —likely inside the Wine Cellar. Cos was meeting with the insurance agent, and Marco, when he learned I was coming, wanted to talk to me about meeting with the same builder we'd used for all of our upgrades, a family friend.

"You okay?" Hudson held my hand.

I nodded, though I wasn't really okay. Tears threatened, but I told myself if he could interrupt his life to get on a plane to be here, I could put on my big-girl panties and do this. Breaking down was not part of today's plan. Too much needed to be done.

"It's gone," I said, knowing I would be crowned the queen of obvious for that statement.

"You are safe. Thayle is safe. And it will be rebuilt."

He must have said that ten times already, and every single time I appreciated it. The reminder snapped me out of my funk.

“I want it exactly as it was before.” I looked away from the burned rubble, having seen enough. “You’re going to freeze. No hat, no gloves?”

“I came directly to your house from work,” Hudson said. “Though now that Mom knows I’m in town, I’ll have to get over there at some point. Maybe you can come with me? Meet the parents?”

I hesitated only because I had no idea what the future held for us. Last night we’d sat on the couch, and after what couldn’t have been more than ten minutes of Hudson rubbing my feet, I was out. The emotional toll of the past two days, not sleeping much . . . it had caught up to me. When I woke up, Hudson at the foot of the couch with my feet still on his lap, we were both covered with blankets.

This morning, after a quick shower and change, we caught my parents for all of five minutes before we left. They were thrilled we planned to head to the estate.

“I’d like that,” I said. “Come on. Let’s get inside.”

We climbed the steps to the Wine Cellar, Hudson only letting go of my hand long enough to open the door. Even though they knew I was coming, Neo and Marco stopped talking and watched us. Cos sat over on the couches with a man I didn't recognize, likely the insurance agent. The floor-to-ceiling fireplace roared, as it was winter, and even without customers, the tasting room was a beautiful sight, which of course made me think of the Barn.

“Is Thayle here?” I asked, approaching the bar. Marco sat behind it, Neo on one of the stools. Both of them had their laptops open.

“She’s downstairs in the cellar with Maci and Peter.”

"Maci is our admin and logistics lead. Peter, the vineyard manager," I explained to Hudson. And then, preemptively, "And before either one of you start any of your shit, I'm not in the mood. Not today."

Hudson chuckled, garnering a glance from both of my brothers.

"Sorry," he said. "I don't see her like this very often."

Neo basically snorted. "Then you don't know the real Min."

"Neo," I warned. Though it seemed he'd said it good-naturedly, I wasn't taking any chances.

Marco watched Hudson carefully but thankfully said nothing.

"Just being honest." Neo stuck out his hand. Hudson took it, and the two shook. "Thanks for coming. And bringing her here this morning."

"No problem," Hudson said, sitting next to me.

"It looks horrific," I said, to no one in particular.

"I know," Marco lamented. "It's hard to look at. To imagine you were in there when the fire started."

I could see Hudson's look of surprise from the corner of my eye. It was understandable. Marco had been a complete asshole to him, so Hudson didn't know the nice side of my brother. It was there. Just hidden deep, deep below the surface.

"Thank god you didn't go looking for the source and ran out of there," Neo said. He shuddered. For him, it must be an especially painful thought, that both Thayle and I were in danger. "I'm glad you came down. We have a lot to discuss."

I sighed, thinking of what we'd just seen. "I didn't want to," I admitted, looking at Hudson. His smile felt like home. There was no other way to say it, and it made no sense. I'd known him for such a short time, but there it was.

"Thanks for coming to New York." All three of us were so surprised by the words from Marco that no one said anything for a second.

"Of course," Hudson said finally.

"Min said you stopped dancing."

"Marco!" I was going to kill him.

"It's okay." Hudson turned toward Marco. "I did. It was time."

I knew that look on Marco's face. He was measuring up Hudson for the first time. He'd dismissed him before, but today was different.

"You're from Brookville?"

"I am."

"Your parents are both in education. Your dad is a superintendent?"

"Marco, can you please not interrogate him?"

Hudson reached over and put his hand on my knee. I took it, and he squeezed.

"You've done your homework," Hudson said, not missing a beat.

"She's my sister," Marco said as if we all didn't know that very fact.

Neo and I exchanged a look, my brother nodding. My parents always tried to figure out our "sibling speak," as they called it, but they were never able. Only I would ever be able to discern Neo's nod, which meant, *let it go*.

"I don't blame you for being protective," Hudson said. "But you're going to figure out eventually that I'm more than a male entertainer your sister had a weekend fling with in Nashville."

"I already have."

Well, if that wasn't the second most shocking comment of the day.

"Although," Marco added, "I still don't see how it will work with you there and Min here."

I was so surprised Marco was coming around and curious enough to want to hear Hudson's answer that I didn't say anything.

"I'd wanted to talk to her privately first." Hudson turned toward me. "When I was in for the wedding, I asked if you'd want me to come home."

"I said yes, obviously."

"You did. Last night you fell asleep, so I didn't get a chance to tell you . . ."

Oh my god. "Are you coming back?"

"I hadn't planned to do this here."

"Hudson," I said, jumping up from the stool. "Are you coming back?"

He answered with a grin that reached his eyes. I threw my arms around his neck, brothers be damned. And frickin' started to cry, again. Screw it. I didn't care. Hudson was coming back. But we had an audience. Thayle joined Neo behind the bar. I wiped my cheeks, with Hudson's help, and stared at him.

"Sooo," Thayle said. "What's going on?"

Half laughing, half crying, I answered, "Hudson is coming back to New York."

Her eyes widened. "No shit? What about your music career?"

I stood next to him, Hudson's broad shoulder tightening under my fingers. Man, my boyfriend was stacked.

Not appropriate at the moment, Min. He's talking about his future here.

"About that, there's more news I was going to tell you

last night," Hudson said, turning to me. "Ray offered me a contract."

My jaw dropped. "What?"

"Ray Spencer."

"I know who you mean, but holy shit, Hudson. That's huge. I don't get it. You said—"

"I thanked him, and turned it down. It wasn't the best deal in the world, and even if it had been . . . I enjoyed singing more when it was a part-time thing. Before it became a job." He shrugged. "It wasn't as much fun anymore."

I must have been crazy to try to talk him into this. "But you were singing covers. These would be your songs. That you could share with the world. It's like night and day."

He didn't seem to be moved. If there was one thing I knew to be true about Hudson, he was as thoughtful a person as I'd ever met. He would never make a decision like this lightly. "It's not for me," he said. "But you are."

"I can't be the girl you gave up a career for," I said, imagining telling this story to our children someday. *Dad could have been a mega superstar but decided to move back to this little ol' town for me instead.*

"I don't look at it as giving up," he said to me, and then to the group who all watched us like this was some sort of movie. The only thing they were missing was the popcorn. "Just fine-tuning my self-discovery. I went down there to see if music could be a job, and for me, it just didn't jibe."

"So what will you do here?" Neo asked.

Good question.

"Tend bar, probably, until I figure that out. Maybe play a gig or two, just to keep the instrument tuned." He addressed my brothers, especially Marco, then. "I know it's not what you'd want for your sister. Some guy with an education degree who never used it, a would-be country singer and former male dancer. But I will love the hell out of Min and treat her like the goddess that she is. I will treat her with respect and earn yours. That's a promise."

Marco's jaw clenched. I held my breath.

He stuck out his hand. "You already have it."

CHAPTER THIRTY

hudson

"It's beautiful down here."

Min turned on the lights, white string ones that gave the private tasting room an otherworldly feel. Wine barrels surrounded us on both sides, with a long dining table and private bar at the other end of the room.

"It's a great spot. Mostly used for small private events or VIP and wine club tastings."

"But you didn't drag me down here for a wine tasting," I said, reaching for her.

"No," Min admitted. "I didn't."

When I kissed her, any doubts I had about the decision I'd made, about the new course my life was about to take, fled to the deepest recesses of my mind. As she opened for me, I tasted only sweetness and love. Acceptance and new beginnings.

Her hands moved to my backside, where they not so subtly squeezed and pulled me closer. If that was how we were going to play it . . . game on.

My hand slipped under Min's soft sweater. I pushed aside the tank top underneath and slid my hand up her back. I unclasped her bra, then brought both hands to the front and pushed the loosened lace bra out of the way.

Min groaned as my hands covered her breasts, and I kissed her harder, letting my thumbs circle her nipples. Min was so goddamn responsive. The memory of her sitting on a chair in Nashville, her hands tied behind her back, made it nearly impossible to stand normally. Straining against my jeans, I pulled away.

"Tonight?" she asked.

My heart skipped a beat at her tone. It wasn't casual at all. It was the tone of a woman who knew what she wanted and was telling me, masked in a question, what would happen between us this night.

"Are you certain?"

"Very certain." Min stepped back, reached under her sweater and, unfortunately, reclasped her bra. "I have to get back upstairs. While I deal with the builder, on your way to get my new phone, can you make a stop at the pharmacy? I'm not on the pill. For obvious reasons."

Dear lord, how would I possibly make it until tonight?

"I'll take care of it. I'll grab some food too and will make you dinner."

"Wait a minute. Are you saying you *cook* too?"

"I'm no Michelin-starred chef, but I know my way around a kitchen."

"Tonight, after, well, you know—"

"After I take your virginity and modesty in one fell swoop?"

"Hudson!"

"Okay, sorry. What were you going to say?"

"I was going to say, after we . . ." She laughed. "Fine, I didn't really have better words for it."

"For a woman who found herself strapped to not one

but two chairs in Nashville, you're surprisingly modest. We'll have to work on that."

"I look forward to it. But seriously, I have to go. I just pulled you down here—" She waved her arms between us. "For this. I'm sorry I fell asleep last night."

"And I'm sorry about the Wine Barn. And for not telling you in private I planned to move back. I'd meant to do it last night, and then this morning you were so nervous about coming here . . ."

"Honestly, I still can't believe it. You are absolutely, one hundred percent sure you want to come back to New York?"

"I am one hundred and twenty percent certain. Now get up there before your brothers change their mind about me and come looking for us."

She didn't move. In all honesty, I didn't want her to. "Can you believe Marco? I nearly fell off my stool."

"It was pretty surprising," I agreed. "Which is why I don't want to ruin it by compromising his sister ten minutes after he shook my hand."

"Fine," Min conceded. "You have everything you need? The receipts for the phone and laptop? The cottage key?"

"I have everything," I reassured her. "I'll be back at the cottage in two hours or so. I'm going to stop by Devine Bakery after my errands. Who knows, maybe I can help them out with some shifts?"

Min tilted her head to the side. "You're going to work at a bakery?"

I pulled her toward me for one last kiss. "I'd work in a sewage treatment plant to come home to this."

She kissed me and then pulled away laughing. "After a shower, of course."

"Of course." Clasping hands, we left the barrel tasting

room. "I have some calls to make this afternoon. Some jobs to quit. But I'll be at the cottage if you need me."

She pulled me to a halt in the doorway. "Are you really going to turn down a music deal to come here?"

"I am going to turn down a music deal because my heart has been telling me for a while I want to make music for fun, not money. I'm moving back to New York because the woman I love, and my family, are here. It makes no sense to stay in Nashville anymore. I'm giving up nothing and gaining everything."

I wasn't sure Min believed me, but she would eventually.

She sighed and reached for the light switch. "I'm still in shock."

The room went dark. "I plan to make my move home the least shocking part of your day. Later, sunshine."

I couldn't see her face but could imagine it.

Something I wouldn't have to imagine in a few hours? Being inside her, making love to her. I just had to manage to get through the rest of the day first.

Though I'd only been here for a total of a few days this past month, I knew where to find the essentials, namely, wood for the fire. My mother's favorite "million-dollar chicken" casserole was in the oven, and I was officially jobless. I'd been able to get both my singing gigs and bartender shifts covered for the next two weeks. So my life in Nashville was done.

I turned down the heat in the shower, knowing I only had fifteen minutes or so until Min was due back. Which was why the creak of an opening door surprised me.

"Hudson?" A second later, the shower door opened.

"You're back early," I said, rinsing the shampoo from my hair.

"Do you usually shower at five o'clock in the afternoon?"

She closed the door, but I could hear the thump of Min's boots landing on the tile. She'd taken off one, and then the second.

"I was at the site," I said. "Stopped by on my way back."

"Why?"

I could see her shadow. Yep, definitely undressing.

"Just wanted to be there. The fire chief cleared it. Figured I'd see if there was anything to be found so you didn't have to go back over."

No response. The shower door opened.

"Jesus, Min."

She stepped inside. Thankfully, the shower was huge, made to accommodate more than one person. It had been built for vacationers, and though this wasn't exactly a vacation, it was about to feel like one.

I pulled her to me, Min squealing as she immediately became soaked. Our mouths melded together under the rainfall shower, our hands seemingly everywhere at once. I wanted to feel every inch of her, and apparently Min wanted the same. She stroked my arms, and then my ass, so I returned the favor. Cupping her, I pressed our bodies together, kissing Min for what seemed both like an eternity and just a few seconds. I could never get enough of this. Reaching down, I slipped first one, and then two, fingers inside her.

"You're wet," I murmured against her lips. "And I don't mean from the water."

When she propped her foot up on a built-in ledge,

giving me even better access, I used it wisely. Kissing her again, my tongue and fingers in tandem, Min's slick body pressed against mine, I concentrated on making her lose control.

"Take me, Hudson."

The very last thing on earth I wanted to do was slip my fingers out, but I also didn't need to be told twice. I ripped open the shower door, and without bothering to dry off, I practically ran into the bedroom, grabbed the pharmacy bag, tore it open, and somehow managed to put on a condom despite the fact that Min just told me to "take her." The words continued to ring in my ears as I made my way back to the shower.

The fresh smell of soap greeted me, as did my girlfriend. But as she reached for me, I could see the worry in her eyes too.

"It'll be okay," I said, not sure what else to say. I had no idea how much this would hurt, so I didn't want to lie and say it wouldn't. Instead, I embraced Min, whose arms wrapped around my shoulders. Kissing her, I tried to make her forget there would be any pain at all. Back in the same position we were in when I left, I said a silent prayer this wouldn't hurt her much, and then I glided myself inside.

Groaning against her lips, the pure pleasure of it . . . Min's tightness nearly my undoing, I stopped when I reached the barrier. And then, I buried myself in her. Min cried out in pain, and I held her tight, cursing under my breath.

To distract her, I kissed her more deeply. My tongue coaxed her into forgetting, and thankfully it wasn't long before she seemed to do just that. Min kissed me back without reserve, her hips beginning to move. And that was the end of me.

She was so fucking tight, I wouldn't last. Pure will and experience holding back were all that allowed me to keep going without exploding. With water running down my back, Dominica now pulling closer, her hands splayed across my ass cheeks, I groaned at the pleasure-pain of it all.

And I began to take her in truth, just as she'd asked.

With every thrust, her lips pressed harder. When my hand inched down between us, Min broke the kiss. She watched me, and I her. Mouth open, I alternately wanted to taste her again and remain where I was. Watching. Marveling. As her head tilted back, I vowed to ensure Min's first time was everything it should be. As she shuddered against me, I held on tight.

"I love you so much," I said, meaning every word.

Her nails dug into the back of my shoulders. Removing my hand, I held on to her, and with one last thrust, found release for the first time inside Min. It was everything I'd imagined, and more. I shuddered, hoping I wasn't squeezing her too tightly.

Eventually, I reluctantly pulled myself away and looked into her eyes. The twinkle there had become so familiar so quickly.

"Give me one sec." Once more I pushed the door open, the bathroom filling with steam, though not nearly as much as the shower had a moment ago, and I quickly took care of the condom and came back to Min. Taking over the bar of soap she'd begun to clean herself with, I finished running it between her thighs.

"Screw that." After lathering my palms, I tossed the bar to the side and used my soapy hands instead.

"Hudson," she said, warning in her voice.

"Yes?" I caressed her breasts, for the sake of washing of course.

"That was insanely delicious." She looked into my eyes. "And I very much want to do it again."

"Good," I said, not leaving a bit of skin untouched.

"But I have one concern."

"Does it still hurt?"

She shook her head. "Isn't there something in the oven?"

Mom's chicken. Our dinner. "Shit."

Her laughter followed me out of the shower and into the bedroom as I tucked a towel around my waist and ran downstairs.

CHAPTER THIRTY-ONE

dominica

"You look like you're going to burst with news. Good, I think?"

I'd just gotten off the phone with Cos as I walked into the kitchen, the smell of bacon and eggs a welcome one this morning.

Two days ago, I hadn't wanted to get out of bed. Today was a totally different story. After waking up in Hudson's arms, I got somewhat dressed, if sweatpants counted as "dressed," and called my brother. Having ignored our group text thread last night, not wanting to chance one or all of my brothers storming into the cottage to see if I was still alive, I finally texted back, asking why there were seven hundred messages in less than twelve hours.

After talking to Cos, now I knew why. Apparently, Neo and Marco had an idea. Last night, they'd gone to Cos and Brooke's house to pitch it, knowing I was unavailable, and here we were. "Bursting with news" was an understatement.

"I love eggs and bacon," I said, "but might have to skip the bacon most days."

"Eggs and toast?"

"Carbs."

"Aren't the enemy. Besides, you look amazing." Hudson motioned for me to come to him, his other hand occupied with the eggs.

I did and earned a not-so-innocent kiss in return.

"If we don't want to burn meal number two . . ." I backed away. "Maybe I'll set the table."

"Sorry about that," Hudson said, his ass looking mighty fine this morning in a pair of gray sweats.

"I'm sure your mother's chicken is amazing, but I'm positive it isn't better than shower sex."

He pretended to think about it. "Her chicken is pretty good."

Laughing, I grabbed my coffee mug after putting down two plates and forks. "Can't be as good as the news I got this morning."

Hudson dished out his eggs onto two plates and then made his way to the microwave. I watched as he patted the bacon with paper towels, wondering how I managed to get so lucky with this guy. It seemed impossible he'd not already been snatched up.

"About the Barn?"

"Nope."

He put two pieces of bacon on my plate and four on his own. "Want more?"

"No, thank you."

"Is it about the vineyard?"

"Sort of. I mean, yes."

"Are you going to make me guess?"

"No, because I'm not going to tell you. My brothers are."

I had his attention now.

Hudson took a bite of bacon, looking confused. "Your brothers?"

"You know, three dark-haired guys who look like they could be cast in a mob movie?"

"Oh, those brothers."

"Oh my god, what did you do to these eggs? They are delicious."

"Ancient family recipe."

"I have ways of finding out," I said.

Hudson groaned. "I am so screwed."

"Not until later. We have to get up to the Cellar. They're on their way there now."

We weren't open yet, but this was a big, like super big, meeting. I could hardly sit in my seat but wanted it to be a surprise.

"Then let's get to it," he said, an entire piece of bacon disappearing into his mouth. One I couldn't stop staring at, thinking what he'd done to me with it last night. "Keep it up, Grado, and we're not going to any Cellar."

"Okay, okay. But seriously," I said between bites. "Thank you, Hudson."

"For?"

"For coming here. For moving back."

"No need to thank me. Wait—" He cocked his head to the side. "As a matter of fact, I do accept thank-yous."

"Of the sexual type?"

"How did you know?"

He winked and took a bite of eggs. We finished eating, Hudson suddenly looking serious.

"Thank you, Min. For giving me such a precious gift last night."

"When I say it was 'my pleasure,' I mean it. Sincerely."

I stood, taking the plates and putting them in the dishwasher. In a flash, Hudson was behind me. I closed my eyes as his body pressed against mine. When he pushed my hair to the side, I tilted my head for better access as Hudson kissed my neck. His lips trailed to below my ear. I still couldn't believe he was here.

Or what Marco was proposing.

"My brothers will be waiting for us," I murmured.

He made a sound of frustration before moving away, gathering our coffee mugs, and putting them into the dishwasher.

"I promise it will be worth it." When he stood back against the counter and crossed his arms, I suddenly remembered when he'd done that once before. "You had that exact same stance in the burlesque bar."

"I call it, 'sexually frustrated,'" he said.

Laughing, I closed the dishwasher. Looking around the kitchen into the wide-open great room, I took a deep breath. "Before you came, I decided to move out of my parents' house. Not that I'm dying to live a stone's throw from my brothers, but it makes the most sense. And will be easy for me . . ." I nearly said us. "To get to work from here. Besides, who passes up a half-a-million-dollar cottage, recently remodeled, on the lake, for free?"

"You're thinking to move here?" he asked.

"I am. Want to shack up with me?"

Hudson didn't miss a beat. "Fuck yeah." He pulled me into him. "What did I do to deserve you?"

"I was thinking the same thing. How were you not snatched up already?"

He looked at me with the most deadpan expression. "I was waiting for you."

Unfortunately, the moment was ruined when the phone rang.

"That would be one of my brothers." I kissed him on the cheek and then walked to my phone. Yep. Marco. He had the least patience of any of us.

"So this is my future, I guess? Being a part of a tight-knit family that also works together?"

If only he knew the half of it.

CHAPTER THIRTY-TWO

hudson

MIN WASN'T KIDDING. WHEN ALL THREE OF THEM STOOD AROUND the tasting bar like they had the day before, it looked as if I were walking into the middle of a godfather movie.

"What the hell took you so long?" Marco said to Min as we took off our jackets.

"Maybe don't ask questions you don't want the answer to," Neo said.

"Hey, Brooke," Min said, pointedly ignoring her brother.

"Hey yourself," Brooke said, looking at Min knowingly. I watched as Min sat on a barstool, trying to figure out what she thought she knew. Min smiled broadly, and though I liked to think I was responsible for her obvious glow, there was something else going on. What was she up to?

I greeted her brothers. They were up to something as well. Cos looked at me thoughtfully, Neo only had eyes for his fiancée, and Marco was actually smiling.

That was a first.

"Min says you're a beer guy," Marco said. Not at all what I'd been expecting.

"I am. Sorry," I said, "wine has just never been my thing."

No one seemed concerned by that. Which was good because I really didn't see the tide turning on that front.

"What do you drink?"

Another odd question, but an easy enough one to answer. "Homestyle IPA at the moment. Bearded Iris is a Nashville brewery, one of my favorites."

"So you're a craft beer guy?"

"I am." And couldn't resist asking, "Why?"

"You mentioned yesterday that you were staying in New York," Cosimo ventured, clearly cautious.

I looked at Min. She didn't hesitate. "I just asked Hudson to move in with me."

"With Mom and Dad," Neo chuckled. "That'll be cozy."

"I'll be taking that cottage after all," Min said. "Looks like we're out on another rent."

"Ooooh . . ." Brooke stood behind the bar with her husband. Leaning against the counter behind her, she crossed her arms. "That's awesome. It's like a little compound."

Marco rolled his eyes. "So awesome," he said, mimicking Brooke's voice. But instead of taking offense, she made a silly face at him. Marco's laugh wasn't something I expected to hear so soon.

"Min says you planned to pick up a shift at Devine? Maybe get a bartending job?"

So that was what this was about. They were worried about my employment situation. I didn't blame them, but that also didn't explain why Min looked so happy.

"I'll get a teaching job if I have to. But if you're worried about me pulling my weight—"

"They're not. Would you guys please get to the point?" Min said, her patience clearly wearing thin.

"Has Min said anything about our plans for an on-site brewery?" Cos asked.

"She has," I confirmed. "That you," I said to Marco, "have been pushing for one. Researching for years. But your parents aren't in favor of it."

"They're coming around," Cos said. "Point is, we've secured Lakeside Construction to rebuild the Barn as soon as the weather breaks. And we all agree now would be the perfect time, while they're on-site, to get the brewery built."

"As much as I want to be there day to day," Marco said, "with everything I do already as VP and as our wholesale manager . . ." He shrugged. "We need someone in there we can trust."

"We want you to manage the brewery," Min blurted.

"I thought I was going to tell him," Marco argued.

"You did," Min said.

"I'm pretty sure you just did."

"I'm pretty sure," Cos said, "the two of you could fight over whether or not there is snow on the ground outside."

"I'd call it ice at this point," Marco said.

"Nope, snow." Min grinned. Everyone in the group laughed. That was, everyone but me.

"A few weeks ago you wanted to kill me," I said, specifically to Marco. "And now you want to entrust me with an idea you've been developing for years?"

Marco's eyes locked on mine.

"It was nothing personal," he said. "My job as her brother"—he put up a hand just as Min started to argue with him—"is to protect her. Even if she doesn't agree. But she doesn't need protection from you."

"By the way," Min added, "that is the closest you'll ever come to hearing an apology from him. Marco doesn't do apologies."

"I would," he argued. "If I was ever wrong."

Everyone groaned. He really was a piece of work. Who was offering me a job. A pretty sweet one too.

There was only one answer.

"You sure you won't get sick of me?" I asked Min. "Living together, working together?"

"Are you kidding me? Not even for a second. They do it." She waved her hand to Cos and Brooke. "And their offices are right next to each other. We'll be in totally separate buildings." She smiled. "Because I'll have a brand-new Barn by then."

That Min smiled while mentioning the Barn was a win to me.

Standing, I reached out to Marco. "I'll gladly manage Grado's new brewery."

He shook my hand as Min squealed. She hugged me, nearly knocking me over.

"Oh, and we have music on Wine Wednesdays. And some other times too. Any time you want to play and grease the ol' singing voice . . ."

"Sounds great," I said sincerely.

"To meet the new timeline," Marco said, "there's a lot to get done. We'll get you on the payroll immediately to start planning."

"And speaking of Wednesdays," Brooke said, "you can only make plans for Wednesday night if it's urgent. You should know that up front."

"Guys, you're freaking him out," Cos said.

I wasn't as much freaked out as overwhelmed. When

Min said her brothers wanted to meet with us this morning, never in my wildest dreams could I have expected this. I'd been prepared to sort things out, figure out what was next for me up here, besides Min. And now I was a part of the family. Or close to it.

"I'm just really grateful," I said. "And slightly surprised, to be honest."

"Just slightly?" Marco asked.

Of all the brothers, he was the one who'd shocked me most. It was like a switch with him. The asshole Min accused him of being—which I wouldn't argue with—had turned it completely around. He smiled good-naturedly now, and the difference in his demeanor was almost startling.

"You're not all that bad," I said, earning a laugh from the others.

"Don't be too sure about that," he teased back as Min hugged him. For all that the two of them fought, their closeness was apparent. And I was a part of this now.

"Welcome to the GVV family," Cos said, pulling a bottle of sparkling wine from the shelf behind him. It looked like Min's namesake to me. "I think it's time for a toast."

Before I knew it, a glass of sparkling wine was in front of me.

"Until the brewery opens," Min teased, "you're going to have to get used to it."

"Open your mind to it," Neo said. "Just see, swirl, sniff, sip, and savor. And voila, you're an expert wine taster."

"I think I'll just skip to the last part." I took a drink.

"So you like it?" Brooke asked.

I didn't want to be rude, knowing Neo created the stuff. But I couldn't outright lie either. "It's better than red."

"Yep," Marco said. "Hudson is definitely our boy for the brewery."

"And for our girl," Brooke added.

I wouldn't argue with either point.

CHAPTER THIRTY-THREE

marco

AND THEN THERE WAS ONE.

As my siblings celebrated, I took the glass of sparkling wine and pulled Min to the side. "Can I talk to you a sec?"

"Sure."

We walked away from the tasting bar toward the other end of the room. As always in the winter, the fireplace had been lit already, so we sat on the couches in front of it.

"Are you okay?"

She nodded, but I wasn't convinced. I knew my sister, and something was still wrong. After seeing how excited she was about hiring Hudson, I thought she'd be on top of the world. And she seemed to be, on the outside. But her eyes told a different story.

"I'm great," she said, but her tone confirmed my suspicions.

"Min," was all I said.

She took a deep breath, gazing at the fire. I was such an idiot sometimes.

"Jesus, I'm sorry. And I brought you over here. I didn't mean—"

"It's fine. I just keep looking at it, imagining every little thing being consumed. It's so scary, how quick the fire spread."

"It'll take time," I said, talking out of my ass. What did I know about recovering from the trauma of losing something as beloved to Min as the Wine Barn? It had been the first building on the estate, and our parents were taking it hard too. Not that I blamed them.

"I know. It's just . . . forcing me to slow down a bit, and you know how I hate that."

"Maybe that's not so bad," I said. "We could all probably use a dose of it." I looked up at the bar, to Neo. "Look what it did to him."

Min laughed, knowing I referred to him and Thayle finally getting together when they took a tour around the lake. Although it was part work too, making connections with vineyard owners and getting ideas to bring back to Grado, the annual wine tour was a rare vacation for whoever did it each year.

"Well, no one will be taking any trips in the near future. Between rebuilding the Barn and a brewery, we'll have our hands full." Min's smile returned. Thankfully. "I still can't believe it's happening. You must be so excited."

"I am. Though Dad is going to pitch a fit."

"Who's telling him?"

Our eyes met. "Cos," we said at the same time.

Min's laughter made me feel a little bit better. She looked toward the bar at Hudson.

"He's a good guy," I said.

"He is. Took you long enough to figure that out."

"Pfft, a few months? I'd say we accepted him pretty quickly."

"After you were a total dick to him."

I shrugged. "I'm a total dick to a lot of people. He's not special."

"First of all, he is special. Second of all, you don't have to be a dick, you know. No one is forcing you to be so suspicious of, well, everyone and everything."

"I'm not suspicious of everyone," I argued, knowing Min was right. It wasn't in my nature to admit it, though.

"Whatever, I'm not going to argue with you."

"For a change."

She waved toward the bar. Unsurprisingly, Hudson joined us a few seconds later. I watched as he sat next to her, his arm going around her shoulders. So little sis finally popped her cherry. At least she did it with a guy like him.

"So how much do you know about brewing beer?" I asked Hudson.

"Not enough to manage a brewery," he said. "I think some research might be necessary."

Min rolled her eyes. "By research you mean drinking with Marco, I assume?"

"Listen," I said to my sister, "it's for the greater good. We don't want to half-ass this thing. If Grado's going to have its own brewery, it needs to be the best one on the lake."

"Why not all of the lakes?" Hudson asked.

"I like the way you think. But Blackmoon Brewery will be hard to top."

"Blackmoon?" Hudson moved even closer to Min, if such a thing were possible. "Don't think I know it."

"It's on the north shore of Keuka." Min looked at Hudson in a way that no woman had ever, or would ever, look at me. Good for them. I was genuinely happy for Min.

"It's only been in business a few years, but their beer is

really good. The vibe of the place is cool too. I'll take you down there to check it out."

"Sounds good," Hudson said. "I have to head back to Nashville next week to get my stuff, but other than that, I'm all yours."

"Why does this whole research idea scare me a bit?" Min asked.

"Because it should," I teased her. It was one of my favorite pastimes. Min had always riled so easily.

"No need to worry," Hudson said. "I'm sure your brother will take care of me."

Min leveled a look at me that came right from Mom's playbook.

"That is exactly what I'm afraid of."

Min might be afraid, but I wasn't. Hudson clearly loved my sister, and that was fine by me. The two of them were perfect together, and I liked the Min he brought out in her. Who would have thought all of this would come out of a bachelorette party in Nashville?

Three of four Grado siblings were now effectively hitched.

As for me? One person for the rest of my life?

No fucking way.

epilogue

Min

"Is it hard, being here? Watching them?"

We sat at a table in one of Hudson's former haunts, Outlaw Ale House. It was like a celebrity had arrived when we'd first come in, with some of his buddies from Encore already here. It was so different being in Nashville with him and not my friends. Last time, it was a weekend-long party. This time, we'd spent two days packing up his stuff, wandering the streets and listening to music. Who knew this town could be as laid-back as it could be party central?

"Not at all," Hudson said as he watched an old friend of his play. "As a matter of fact, it's validating."

"Anyone need a beer?" Oliver asked. Hudson said he did.

"No, thanks," I said, thrilled to hear a song I knew. I liked country music but just didn't listen to it a lot. "I have to listen to this stuff more often."

"Maybe I can sing it for you at the estate?"

"Seriously?" Hudson had previously said he needed to think about jumping back into singing, even for Grado.

"I think once a week or two would be perfect, if you guys are still open to it?"

"I don't want it to feel like a job," I said. Our eyes caught. I swallowed. He was thinking dirty thoughts, I could tell.

"I'm suddenly feeling a little tired," he said despite not looking tired at all.

"Me too. Jet lag maybe."

He laughed. "From a one-hour time difference?"

We got up at the same time. "Hold that beer," Hudson told Oliver as we passed him and Dominic at the bar. "I'll catch you guys tomorrow at the show."

For our last night in Nashville, we were going to Encore. The minute Oliver found out Hudson was coming back to pack his stuff, he begged him to dance one final time. At first Hudson said no, but when I found out, I insisted. But only if he wore his cowboy outfit. And only gave me a lap dance, of course.

"I might get kicked out of the show for the things I plan to do to you," Hudson whispered to me.

"Sounds good," Donny said. "See you then."

We practically ran the few blocks to his apartment. The second we got inside, Hudson didn't hesitate. He lifted me up and carried me into the kitchen, of all places. But when he kicked a chair away from the table and put me in it, I suddenly realized why.

I may have told him that private dances were always welcome. Sure enough, he pressed a few buttons on his phone and another country song began to play. Since he always wore his boots and belt, it wasn't far off the mark to say that I was getting my cowboy dance one day early.

Hudson began to move, unbuttoning his flannel shirt one button at a time. When he pulled off his boots and socks, Hudson wearing only jeans now, my pulse quickened. I remembered wanting to touch those abs so badly, first at the club and then during our private dance at the house. This time, my hands weren't tied. I reached out and indulged, Hudson groaning at the touch. He straddled me then and began to circle my hips.

His kiss wasn't gentle.

In seconds I was consumed, his tongue teasing and swirling as his hips continued to work their magic. I reached between us and tried to get his buckle off. When I couldn't, Hudson broke away. Standing, he did it for me.

No way I could continue to sit and watch him undress. Pulling off my shirt and tossing my own boots and socks to the side, I squealed as Hudson reached for me. Running into his bedroom, the rest of my clothes leaving a trail behind me, I jumped onto his bed.

By the time he stood in the doorway, he was ready. And so was I.

"Fuck," he said. I may have also let slip that I loved how Geralt, aka Henry Cavill, said that in *The Witcher*. Now Hudson used the curse in that deep voice every chance he got. And I was here for it.

By the time he pressed inside me, I was nearly ready without any more priming. When Hudson flipped us over, reaching down between us, I didn't go easy. Our frantic pace matched each other's, and it wasn't long at all before I cried his name, my head tilting back as another way to release the built-up tension. Hudson held my hips in place as he came too, my name on his lips a sweet sound I'd never get tired of hearing.

I collapsed on him, spent. Happy. Blissful, in fact.

"Like I said . . ."

"Fuck," I finished, imitating his deep tone. We both laughed.

"Could you ever have imagined," I said, rolling onto my back next to him, "that first night? That we'd be back in your apartment, packing your stuff to move back to New York? To move in with me?"

"I can safely say no. Especially since I thought you were engaged."

"I still don't think you noticed me that night."

Hudson rolled onto his side, his head propped on his hand. He looked me straight in the eyes. "I noticed you, Min. The first night at Encore. At the bar when you were texting me . . ."

"Not knowing I was texting you."

"Think about it. If Aunt Dorothy hadn't given you my number—"

"Or Brooke hadn't left."

"Or if you'd chosen anywhere but Nashville to have the bachelorette party."

"Do you believe in fate?" I asked, genuinely curious. "Or do you think it's just a string of coincidences that brought us together?"

Hudson thought about it for a second. "I'm not sure, to be honest. I think there are arguments to both sides. But I do think the energy we create ultimately comes back to us, and the more we realize that, the more obvious it is."

"I honestly have no idea what you're talking about right now."

Hudson laughed. "You light up a room, Min. You smile, you welcome others. It was so easy for me to be attracted to you, and not just in a physical way. It was impossible for me to ignore you. Your positive energy pulled me in and never let go."

"So 'sort of' fate but not really?"

"Exactly."

"I'm still confused."

Laughing, Hudson pulled me toward him. "Ultimately, it doesn't matter. We found each other, and I am never, ever letting you go."

"Same. I love you, cowboy."

"I love you too," he said, and kissed my nose, "sunshine."

How does a guy like Hudson propose to the woman he loves? Become a Grado Valley Vineyards VIP to read a *Sip & Savor* bonus scene at BellaMichaels.com/Insider.

Then get ready for more Grado Valley Vineyards goodness with Marco's story in *Horizontal Tasting.*

also by bella michaels

Boys of Bridgewater

Overruled by Love

Last Call

Billion Dollar Date

My Foolish Heart

Grado Valley Vineyards

Pop and Pour

Lay It Down

Sip and Savor

Horizontal Tasting

about the author

Bella Michaels is the pen name of a contemporary romance author. While not writing historical romance as Cecelia Mecca and steamy small town as Bella, she loves dreaming up new sassy heroines and alpha heroes for readers to enjoy. Firmly for Gryffindor and House Stark, she lives with her husband and two teens in Pennsylvania.

Sign up to be a Bella Michael's Insider to receive bonuses and updates via email at BellaMichaels.com/bonus or by using the QR code below:

Made in the USA
Columbia, SC
16 July 2024

38713027R00131